£1.99

HUNGRY LIKE THE WOLF

John Crawford

DEDICATION

To the Clan:
Mom, Dad, Mark, Paul, Pete, Annie, Sarah

PROLOGUE

When the staff and students at the Tolkien College of Education and Continuing Studies stopped for a minute, and thought long and hard about it, it seemed - now that they had time to think long and hard about it - that maybe it had been obvious from the start that there was something a little amiss about Maddox.

Apart from him being a serial killer that is.

What happened to the two lads had gone far beyond what was considered right. Boys will be boys someone said - no one said they had it coming - no one thought they deserved it.

Sandra swore blind she'd heard at least three ribs crack when one of the lads fooled around with a puppy at the end-of-year barbecue.

Even though she'd had four glasses of rum punch and a Raspberry Daiquiri, it still seemed as if he was only messing around with the little dog, scuffling its ears, and tickling its tummy. She remembered it well - it was by the far end of the flagstones, between the stone pillars, just beyond that

1

bit which sinks down into the landscaped square with the all-season borders.

It was like someone snapping a Kit-Kat.

"The poor thing yelped like you wouldn't believe," said Sandra. "He claimed the puppy had burned his mouth on a kebab, or scorched himself on one of Eileen's hot dogs."

"I don't think Eileen puts enough onions on her hot dogs," Val said, wondering why Eileen didn't let everyone just help themselves to the onions.

Mary said that she once came across one of the lads treading a tropical fish into the carpet. There he was dancing on a Neon Tetra for all he was worth. The boy said he had found the fish flapping around on the floor, blaming its escape from the tank on whoever changed the water.

"He said he was putting it out of its misery."

"By putting it out on the carpet?"

"And the mess! They're only little, those fish, but the guts on them. Squished all over the place!"

Even so, boys will be boys someone said again - no way did they deserve what happened to them.

Grumpy old Frank from the basement stores never had any time for Maddox despite just about everyone going on about him being a grand chap and all.

Frank could see right through him all right. He was an excellent judge of character, was Frank. There was no great mystery there - Maddox was a nasty piece of work all right. All smiling and nice and friendly to your face - you cross him though and you were done for.

Even now, he could feel his throat gulp as he recalled those scalding green eyes ripping through him after he had delivered the wrong prospectuses to a classroom. He never scared me, mind, Frank told Ross, the young trainee, who looked up from his newspaper, eager to hear more. Ross had never worked anywhere before with such an association to murder - and by one of the nicest chaps you could wish to meet too.

"I always liked him," said Ross. "He told me I had the best ear lobes in the college."

"I kept all the newspaper clippings," said Frank, pulling out a ring binder and flapping it open. "A terrible business. The thing with the dogs was bad enough but what he did to the others on the team-building week would turn your stomach for sure."

Frank unclipped a cutting and handed it to Ross.

"This was the church service - they asked for a recent photo. That's him, just turning away from the camera - you can see he's smiling."

Ross had already heard about how Maddox had walked out on his wedding to that dippy girl Alice from Admin.

On the day in question, Michael Maddox had been standing at the altar with the priest just in front of him. Alice Bullard - soon to be Mrs Maddox - looked radiant as she moved down the aisle on the arm of her father, Alan. Her glossy black hair was piled up high, glittering with blue highlights - spiralling curls were expertly teased around rosy cheeks to frame her happy, glowing features. Her eyebrows, artfully plucked and arched to perfection, acknowledged each reassuring smile from the pews. How she wished she could have glided down the aisle but Alice wasn't given to gliding, never having been the most graceful of girls but she certainly glowed. The little garlands of lilies and chrysanthemums at the end of each pew dropped petals like confetti. Confetti that remained tightly boxed in their little glossy containers when the priest said to Maddox:

"Wilt thou have this woman to thy wedded wife?"

"No," Maddox said. "Actually I'd rather not."

Maddox then turned quickly on his heel and walked straight back up the aisle. Even during his leaving, he was pleasant and courteous to all the guests as he passed them in the pews. He graciously nodded to the Hanburys who were gathered in a central pew, and gave a little wave to old

Mrs Romney who responded with a tight little flutter of her own. Jackie, her hair severely constrained within a wide-brimmed bonnet and pinned within an inch of its life, expressed such an air of wide-eyed consternation, one would have thought she'd been practising for weeks. The pews were rattling and rustling with assorted gasps and splutters. Mrs Postans said that Maddox had been particularly attentive to her when he left as she'd arranged the flowers and the table centrepieces.

Maddox pushed through the heavy church doors and walked over to the small gravelled car park where he climbed into the Ford Focus that he had used that very morning to ferry Mrs Postans and her floral tributes to church. After adjusting his seat belt, and carefully checking the mirror, he calmly drove off by himself to the airport. It was from here where, armed with passport, flight tickets, credit cards, and two rather thin novels, he boarded a flight to the Canary Islands and enjoyed, all in all, a very pleasant honeymoon without his wife-to-be on the sandy shores of Gran Canaria.

Alice's father had been apoplectic with rage, going quite red in the face. More of a deep scarlet, bordering on a vermillion, Mary would have said - and she should know, what with her working in the Art Department and having recourse to all those colour swatches.

Alan had really wanted to smack him one. His daughter humiliated like this, the poor girl left standing in front of the altar by herself, not sure what to do with the bouquet as she plucked at the petals and let them fall to the floor.

The priest said he'd never known the like, and by the time Alan had fought his way to the back of the church, Maddox was long gone.

"I'll kill him! For what he's done to Alice, I'll kill him!"

Maddox stayed at a luxurious hotel overlooking the sand dunes, in the suite booked for the honeymoon, and readily paid the surcharges without offering exhausting explanations to the receptionist.

When he returned after a refreshing fortnight and a fairly decent tan, he was having a quiet drink in the Horse and Jockey, when the pub door opened, and Alan walked in and smacked him one.

Pat the barman said, "Outside, both of you! Now, now lads! Leave it out!" and other such sundries.

"It wouldn't have happened if this moose hadn't jilted my daughter at the altar!" said Alan.

It was true - Alice had been jilted good and proper.

After the initial shock, the requisite umbrage taken, and a fair to middling shedding of tears, Alice had returned to the house with a tattered bouquet where her mother, Jean, prepared herself for a bit of tender counselling and I told you sos.

Only she had nothing worth telling of the telling you so variety. Jean had genuinely liked Maddox - he was usually always decent, courteous and attentive to Alice. Poor old Alice who could never have believed she would ever in a million years have attracted the attentions of someone so seemingly suitable.

Back at the house, the debacle at the altar had been discussed up in Alice's old room. She wondered about throwing herself into the pillows with a howling display of heart-rending wretchedness, but decided against it.

Her mother came back up the stairs with a nice hot cup of tea. Alice had resisted shrugging off the wedding dress, an ivory confection with creamy-yellow straps and assorted frills. The fine stockings and the exquisite cream slip had cost a bomb; the pearls she had borrowed from an ancient aunt, and the brand new matching gloves were now irredeemably tear-stained. Her blue shoes, she felt, were a little too high in the heel but Alice always had problems with shoes. She kicked them off, and looked across the room at her reflection in the dressing table mirror. It cut too tragic a figure to lose so soon, especially with the running mascara giving her the look of a stunned raccoon.

"I didn't like him anyway," Jean said, "and neither did Alan or Simon."

"Mommy - you all adored him!" shrieked Alice.

Hearing the front door bell, Alice stood up sharply. Her mother went downstairs and stood by the door, unsure of what to do.

Leaning over the bannister, Alice saw her brother Simon walk along the hallway, munching on an apple.

"Simon, open that door!" she said.

Simon shrugged and moved towards the front door. Jean stood to one side of a small table, wringing her hands, and taking tiny little steps from one foot to the other as if desperate for a pee.

"If it's Michael, tell him I never want to see him ever again." Alice wailed.

"I'll send him away with a flea in his ear," Jean said. It was a saying she'd been dying to use since hearing it on Coronation Street. But still she clutched her hands and dithered on the spot.

The bell chimed again. Just as Simon reached for the latch there was a rattle of keys and the door opened.

"Alan!"

"Sorry. Thought I'd forgotten my key but it was in my inside pocket all along. I couldn't find the bastard. How's Alice?"

"I don't like you using that sort of language in the house, Alan," said Jean.

Alice retreated quickly to her room and rubbed her eyes, massaging a fresh puffiness beneath each eye. Her lipstick (Crushed Flamingo) was smeared, and she was on her way down for a bit more sympathy when the bell rang again.

It was David - Simon's best friend from college.

"Alright mate, come through."

Alice heard a tinny clunk as Simon tossed his apple core into the wastebasket.

"Hello David, love, would you like a nice hot cup of tea?" Jean said.

"No thanks Mrs B."

Alice rushed back upstairs to the bathroom and quickly washed her face, repeatedly splashing cold water over her bloodshot eyes. She managed to repair a little of the damage, and then quickly shrugged off her wedding dress. Flailing through her old wardrobe, she settled on a loose teal-coloured T-shirt and a pair of faded blue jeans, which she considered her most complementary casual ensemble. There was still something about David that elicited this response in her, and even now, she still found it a little disquieting - a little unsettling and confusing. That tiny jolt she got in the pit of her stomach whenever she saw David pranged her again as she walked down the stairs and saw him standing there with Simon. Here on her wedding day - or non-wedding day as it happened. Whatever was the matter with her?

Simon and David walked into the back room and pushed the door shut behind them.

"Fancy forgetting your key," said Jean.

"I didn't forget it - I just forgot where I put it."

"Did you not see Michael then."

"No, he's done a runner for sure. But mark this, I'll leather him when I catch him. Doing that to our Alice. In front of all those people too - the humiliation!"

Jean switched on the hall light and went into the lounge, instinctively allowing the boys their own space in the back room. Alan shook his head and followed his wife through to the lounge, settling down in the chunky black leather chair with the adjustable foot-rest. Maybe he would go down to the Horse and Jockey later. Alice looked at the closed door of the back room, and went back upstairs.

"Cup of tea, love?"

7

Alan nodded almost imperceptibly, a lizard gulp.

"I tell you, I am going to leather him. He can't do what he did to our Alice and get away with it."

"I just don't understand why he did it. It seems so out of character for Michael to do such a thing. Do you think he had a mental turn or something?"

"He'll be getting one from me and that's for sure."

"I'll put the kettle on! Did he say why he ran off?"

"I told you, he'd gone by the time I got outside."

"Outside now!" Pat the barman came swiftly round from behind the counter, a damp cloth draped over a shoulder and a fixed look of grim determination on his shiny scrubbed face.

Maddox pulled himself up, using the spilled chairs on either side of him. He finished his beer with a flourish, checked out his features in the mirrored stand of a beer-pull, and asked in all sincerity what it was he'd done to warrant such an unprovoked attack.

When he picked himself up again, there was a strange glint to Maddox's eyes, little glittering slits that in an instant folded open to an almost childlike innocence.

A young couple sitting on the long leather bench bum-walked further along their seat, jiggling their drinks as they went along. The young man then bumped his way back down to retrieve a packet of crisps from the table. If the pub had not been so quiet in the first place, there would have been a sudden silence followed by hushed exclamations, but the two punches visited upon Maddox served only to stir Pat the barman. The fists had hardly stirred Maddox at all. Apart from those eyes of course.

"And stay away from Alice. If I ever see you anywhere near her again, you'll know about it!"

Alan's body was never found. It certainly hadn't turned up with the other corpses - the ones bloated and greasy and buttery from having spent so much time under water. The things he'd done to them didn't bear thinking about - much to Ross's disappointment as he was all for the bearing of such thoughts.

An intercom buzzer blared and the shutters to the basement doors began to roll up. Frank took another long drag on his cigarette as he watched a van pull in to deliver a pallet of copier paper. He flicked the nub out onto the loading bay, and snapped the binder shut. A bright wedge of sunlight spooled across the forecourt.

"The strangest thing," Frank said, squinting in the glare of the sudden sunlight. "Maddox really didn't think he'd done anything wrong - not really. Nothing wrong at all."

PART ONE

CHAPTER ONE

Alice's engagement to Michael Maddox followed a summary courtship that had quite baffled the pair of them. For Alice, it was the by-product of (at least to her) an eventual acceptance of her unrequited love for another being exactly that - unrequited.

Despite playing 'I Will Always Love You' on a continual loop, and turning her hand to some flowery if ineffectual poetry, the realisation finally sank in that it just wasn't going to happen.

At first, Alice had felt a numb kind of pressure, swiftly escalating into a crushing revelation when she found out whom her longed-for suitor was involved with. She recalled how she had actually trembled - quivered like some shivery shaking thing when it all became clear.

Then the resignation began to set in - she was sure there had even been a sigh.

Alice was good at resignation.

Alice and Maddox had a peculiar beginning to their relationship, there being little in the way of a compelling attraction when first they met. With his thin lop-sided smile and prominent eye-tooth, Maddox created an impression of beguiling self-possession. An enigmatic aura, it was generally agreed, had him well catered for.

They went for a drink together and then onto a small Italian restaurant in the Jewellery Quarter, sharing Gnocchi Alla Portofino from the same dish. The following week, they went to see the latest James Bond film. Within a few weeks, they were emerging from the cinema hand in hand and, on one particular weekend, Mary spotted them with their arms around each other. They were under an umbrella even though it wasn't raining particularly hard. More of a grey drizzle, Mary would have said.

Maddox would gently tease Alice about her sweet tooth - a meal never went by without her ordering a strawberry scoop or the sundae with chopped nuts. At the cinema, at least two little tubs of vanilla would be purchased with coffee before they went in to see the film.

Alice often sucked ice cubes – her mother's reliable remedy for anxiety – they cooled her mouth and fetched up chillingly against her back teeth.

She would feign exasperation at Maddox's blistering intelligence - particularly his habit of commenting on every film they watched with little asides and appendices of his own, his discourses moving effortlessly between critical theories and trite observations.

Maddox's cinema leanings did not favour French post-war cultural films or realist documentaries, as Alice may have expected, but Hollywood blockbusters and poorly-reviewed gore epics.

Alice hardly blinked during the horror screenings, unlike some of the frothy, young girls who yelped at the slightest sight of blood. If anything, she laughed at the ridiculousness of it all. Horror was comedy, an interchangeable theme that

11

would have her howling with laughter as a bodiless head tumbled down a stairwell, or a squirming mass of maggots came gushing out of empty eye sockets.

"How can you not laugh at a decapitated head bouncing down some church steps?" Alice once asked during a zombie feature. "Although I do take issue with the sound effects. Surely a series of dull thuds would work better than all that clanging."

There was no noticeable tingle, no pummelling electricity like she had experienced before, there was nevertheless a gentle, pleasing companionship with Maddox which soon gave cause for her hand to fall into his during a routine on-screen flaying.

It was almost as if their hesitant courtship was nothing more than the conclusion to a string of natural events and mutual groomings. And Maddox was good at conclusions.

When Maddox first turned up for the interview at the college, the principal, Mr Richardson, said to him:

"Here at Tolkien College, we feel more impetus is needed on our English Literature modules and we're looking for someone to crank it up a notch or so."

Principal Richardson had at one time a thick head of hair. On the shelf behind him, an early family portrait showed him possessing a goodly amount of ginger thatch. A framed certificate on the wall by the window declared that he had racked up the most species of birds seen during the local Ornithology Club's Bird-athon.

For his own part, Principal Richardson appraised Maddox just as thoroughly - the tall and dark duly noted - the handsome seeping through in its own time.

Full head of hair, a nondescript nose - and let's face it, nondescript is exactly the sort of nose most people would strive for. Well defined eyebrows without any of those rebellious wiry bristles that begin to loop out of the mix at a certain age.

12

Being a vain sort of chap, Principal Richardson mentally ticked away Maddox's physiognomy as if it were a list of elusive warblers. He didn't envy the hair despite being bald himself - hair had never really suited him no matter how it was styled - it was the brows he coveted, his own being fair and insubstantial - quite weedy by comparison.

But it was those eyes and the fox-like grin that did for Principal Richardson. Green eyes of no particular hue, no searing emerald or winsome jade, probably as nondescript as the nose yet put to work in so many different ways. Maddox seemed to expand and dilate his pupils at will, flooding them with black or pulling them back to scarcely detectable pinpricks.

Not fox-like either, Principal Richardson decided later on when all he could think about was that extraordinary smile. More wolfish - or even the grin of a jackal. Do jackals smile? Or foxes come to that. No, it was the smile of a wolf, accentuated by that slightly elongated eyetooth, a canine that pulled the symmetry from his face.

"It's not that we want to stray from the syllabus. That's not what we want at all," Principal Richardson continued.

"Keeping to the syllabus naturally," Maddox said, "but taking up the slack - tucking in the ends so to speak."

"Exactly," said Principal Richardson. "We must have room to grow on these modules. They are tight enough as it is."

"Of course."

"You understand that we can't come to any decision straight away. We have other candidates to see."

Maddox was a study in equanimity although he managed to exude a wintry complicity that reeled in Principal Richardson.

"I think I could be just what you're looking for," he said.

At the second interview, Principal Richardson poured some tea, added milk, and handed the cup and saucer over to Maddox.

"So it was definitely a spoonbill? You're absolutely sure?"

"I think so - it was standing on the edge of a pool."

"Down in Dorset, you say?"

"Yes - Weymouth. The next reserve along from Radipole Lake. I can't quite recall its name – Lodmoor, I think."

"Not an egret?"

"No."

Maddox was slowly pacing around Principal Richardson's office, sliding his hand along the bookshelves, plucking out the occasional volume and running his bony fingers over the cover as if to absorb its contents.

"You'll find Tolkien College quite unlike other institutions of education." Principal Richardson explained. "The emphasis being as much on involvement as achievement. The taking part is the very crux of the Tolkien philosophy."

"The very crux," repeated Maddox.

Principal Richardson glanced at Maddox, unsure of the sincerity with which this last remark was spoken but Maddox had assumed a kindly expression - a kindly expression tempered by that formidable eyetooth.

"The post, as such, is a new one," Principal Richardson continued. "We already have a Director of English Language and Literature - Jonathan Mortimer. He needs a deputy, and your role would support the itinerary as the modules progress. The semester does include a reading week - perhaps there will be an opportunity there for you to suggest an alternative for the students?"

Maddox sat down and took a swig of his tea.

"Hobnob?"

"Thank you."

Maddox swivelled around on his seat, an arm draped along the back of the chair, long fingers drumming on the upholstery.

"Yes, I think I'll be very happy here," he said, "I take it you will offer me the position?"

After a few weeks settling into his new position at the college, Maddox secured an apartment just outside the city centre. As he strolled through the aisles at the local supermarket, he found himself approving of the tightly packed produce, and the neatly arranged shelves with their coloured boxes and bottles.

So many varieties of tuna - Tomato & Herb, Thousand Island Dressing, Spicy Salsa, Coronation, Mustard, Lemon (didn't fancy that one much), Three Bean Salad and Thai - all perfectly ranged along their respective shelves.

Maddox chose two tins of the Tomato and Herb, laying the flat tins down in his basket so that they lined up with the punnet of cherry tomatoes, the thick wedge of Gouda and the loaf of Super Toastie.

The store was getting crowded with students from the nearby university, the grounds of which tumbled down from the main quad and clock tower. Built on a campus model and incorporating a medical school, the university was a short journey away from Tolkien College with which it was affiliated, and provided the mainstay of lodgers and roomers in the area.

Maddox attached himself to the 8 items or fewer queue, just behind an older man and a gaggle of students, which included a couple of scruffy lads and a rather posh girl with pink sprayed hair. The man left the queue to fetch some forgotten item, and returned back to his place in front of the group. Maddox expected some sort of fuss but there was none. Perhaps the younger generation was becoming more tolerant.

The posh girl behind him, her clipped vowels incongruous when allayed to the slouched ones of her pasty companions, was gushing about the other night at the guild bar where some of her friends had, like, an incredible, like, time and, like, it was really, like, awesome, like.

Crossing the busy main road, Maddox made his way to his rented accommodation in one of the huge Victorian houses that lay behind the fire station. The sweep of this residential street curled away from the cheaper student accommodation and the shared houses of the terraced properties that branched off from the main road.

The little self-contained flat took up the whole of the second floor, comprising of a sizeable bedroom, and a spacious lounge with a small kitchen area.

Maddox unpacked his shopping, laying the various items onto the kitchen counter, which was a little low for his height. Where part of the ceiling sloped down to a dormer window, there was a wooden desk. He thought he might move the desk over to the larger window that overlooked the long garden at the back.

Looking out, he could see a black cat sprawled out on top of the garden shed, luxuriating in a slice of late afternoon sunlight as only cats can. Beyond the long lawn lay the back gardens of the tall houses opposite, and all their attendant debris - sheds, mowers, rakes and broken barbecues - an empty swing dangled listlessly, surrounded by plastic toys.

A single tree, a fir or pine - something coniferous - dominated the view from the main window. His landlady, Mrs Wardroper, said it would be chopped down soon, which seemed a shame to Maddox who had noticed many birds perched amongst its branches.

He hadn't a clue what species of bird they were, and his eyes momentarily drifted to the Book of British Birds that he'd bought for the second interview.

Maybe he would look them up later. Or maybe not.

It was Val who had recommended these rooms - she was the manager of the main college office on the second floor, which dealt with admissions and accommodation. The rooms she suggested were out of the price range of most students - apart from the rich overseas intake, and a few were retained for the lecturers or the wealthier post-graduates.

Most of his belongings were still scrunched up in the two

holdalls and black leather sports bag by the side of the bed. He had most of his possessions in storage, which he would arrange to be delivered later. The holdalls were zipped tight and bulged with clothes and linen. The leather bag peeled back to reveal a small selection of books, and a sizeable canvas pouch, which clinked when Maddox rolled it to one side.

He pulled out his shirts and two pairs of trousers, carefully hanging them up. The old wardrobe was sturdily made with smooth dovetailing and a brass rail running along the base - presumably to keep shoes neatly lined up. Maddox couldn't think what else you could use it for.

Changing into his slippers, he checked the soles of his leather shoes and placed them in the wardrobe.

Mrs Wardroper said she was planning to replace the wardrobe with more up to date furniture but Maddox said he hoped she wouldn't - it was easily the most interesting piece in the apartment with its little compartments and shelving.

There was a section dedicated to socks, another for underwear and T-shirts. A narrow shelf set back was ideal for housing deodorants and sprays.

However, the tie rack was not really required as he only owned two ties - a functional dark blue tie for weddings, funerals and interviews, and a woven polyester scarlet tie.

The scarlet tie was particularly good for strangling.

CHAPTER TWO

Alice thought back to the time when Maddox first arrived at Tolkien College.

The appointment of the good-looking and somewhat enigmatic Assistant Director to the Department of English Language and Literature had created a bit of a stir at the time. Her heart, as she recalled, was set elsewhere - as were her thoughts. However, she did recall an earlier conversation about Maddox with Gill, the scatty, dressed-far-too-young-for-her-age colleague who lectured on creative writing.

"I don't quite know what you mean by unusual?" Alice had said.

"Not unusual - more a bit different," said Gill.

"In what way?"

"I don't know really. Mysterious I suppose."

Alice couldn't see it herself but she was too wrapped up in her own beleaguered love life to notice much going on within the college. She caught herself thinking of her new 'boyfriend' (it needed the inverted commas) - was he really so young? Or did he just look young? Too young for her is what she meant.

"Yes, not cloaked in mystery like in the books but, you know, sort of mysterious and not mysterious at the same time," Gill picked up a paper clip and began to unwind it, "which kind of comes down to this total semi-mysterious man which is so fascinating."

Alice could see why Gill was teaching creative writing.

The next day:

"He's sort of asked me out," said Gill.

"Is there such a thing as sort of asking someone out?" asked Alice, discovering that she suddenly wasn't very keen on the idea.

Gill was slim, attractive and a bit mad with tiny faded blue tattoos running up her forearms, and the most mesmerising red hair Alice had ever seen. Indeed, she was particularly proud of her hair ("It's not strawberry blonde - its fuckin' ginger!"), which she wore up at work but would unleash to the elements as soon as she left college - more often than not at the Slaughtered Dugong across the road.

Once a year she would return from some exotic trip abroad, glowing with anecdotes and shiny from the sun.

"I told him I was hoping to go to Brazil and he seemed to know all about the place. Things went from there and he mentioned we should maybe get together sometime and have a bit of a chat."

"A bit of a chat," said Alice.

"Maybe even a bit of a day out - a ramble and pub lunch. He seemed quite keen on a canal walk - I asked if he fancied going this weekend and he was all for it."

"So you asked him out?"

"We sort of asked each other out, I guess."

How Alice wished she had the nerve to sort of ask someone out. Especially that 'one' with the inverted commas.

She was not surprised that Maddox knew about Brazil - he seemed to know an awful lot about a lot of things.

It also came as no surprise that Gill had asked him out. She did not dislike Gill but found her self-assurance and confidence was in stark contrast to Alice's own natural reticence and, if she was being honest, a trickle of envy had spilled into her.

"I thought Sandra was quite taken with Michael," said Alice, indicating Sandra's recently vacated chair in the office.

As this was said for no other reason than to mischievously see how she reacted, Gill didn't disappoint.

"No - no way! He's not Sandra's type at all! And she's far too young!"

Gill continued to straighten another paper clip, and began to explore a fingernail with it.

"He's so funny as well. Michael really knows how to make you laugh."

"I'd not noticed," said Alice and she hadn't.

"In the wetlands of Brazil," said Maddox, "you may see a capybara - they are the biggest rats in the world."

Gill laughed her laugh, a guffaw that rattled around her throat before finding its way out.

"It's true," said Maddox. "They are the size of a small pony."

Gill finished her throaty laugh and then lit up another cigarette.

"I should quite like to see a rat that big - it must be quite a sight," he said.

"You're joking, of course!"

"Not a bit of it - I wish I could go with you."

So do I, thought Gill.

It was Saturday and, at Maddox's suggestion, Gill had met him off the train and they had gone for a short walk along the canal with the promise of a pub lunch to follow. Gill would have preferred a wine bar in the city centre but happily agreed to some fresh air if it meant a few hours in the company of Maddox.

She was a little surprised when he turned up at the station in his Ford Focus.

"Hop in," he said.

"I thought you were meeting me off the train."

"That's what I've just done."

"It's just that I expected you to come by train too."

Gill gazed at him as he pushed open the car door. She caught her own look in the side mirror like a baffled thrush listening for worms.

"If I knew you were driving, I could have come with you in the first instance," she said.

"Yes, you could have." Maddox said, slotting back his seat belt and checking the overhead mirror. To look at himself or to check for traffic, Gill wasn't sure.

Maddox slipped a disc into the drive and Freddie Mercury was suddenly telling them that he had just killed a man.

"I love this one," Gill said as Maddox pulled out onto the quiet road. With his arm hanging out of the open window, he drummed his long bony fingers to the tempo of the song.

"I quite like this one too," Maddox said as Queen finished and a classical piece took up.

"Mozart's Horn Concerto in E Flat Minor - a stunning arrangement. I used to get this one confused with his Horn Concerto in F but it's totally different if you listen carefully."

As his long sweeping fingers swished and sashayed to the horns, Gill waited for the next song in the mix. She wasn't expecting Nirvana.

"I love a good ballad," she said.

They had driven only a short while before pulling into the car park of a canal side pub with a large beer garden that had been beefed up with weeping willows and towering pampas. Maddox switched off the engine, and Gill climbed out, immediately eyeing an empty table on the edge of the lawn.

"We can walk from here," Maddox said. "It's only over that stile and onto the canal."

Gill would have preferred to eat at the pub and dispense with the walk altogether.

Although keen to trek over mad places in Indonesia, or to pootle around Marrakesh, she couldn't abide the tweeness and gentility of England's green and pleasant land. There was no pleasure in exploring her own country - if she heard one more person going on about the over-rated merits of Cornwall or the bleedin' Lake District, she'd have one. As far as her own country was concerned, its merits stretched to pubs, chips and real ale.

The towpath was all but deserted apart from the occasional jogger or cyclist trundling past. Gill pulled her usually fast gait into line with Maddox's easy saunter.

"This is great," she said. "I love the countryside."

Walking aimlessly a few hundred yards behind them, unnoticed by either Maddox or Gill, two youths scuffled along the towpath, stopping every now and again to kick an old tin can or throw stones into the water.

"I'm bored," said one of the youths.

"You're always fuckin' bored," said the other.

Maddox and Gill came to a section of the canal that cut deep into the side of a bank, creating a turning area for barges and narrow boats. There were no vessels in sight but a pair of swans spun around in the water, hissing at a little yapping terrier on the bank.

"Swans," said Maddox.

"You know so much about stuff - birds and things and capybaras," said Gill, looping her arm through his.

She rattled out another throaty laugh as they inched past the frenzied little terrier.

22

"What a lot of fuss from such a little fellow!" she laughed.

The incessant yapping faded to a yip as they strolled further on, pushing past tired vegetation that would, in time, overgrow the towpath. They reached a lock and Maddox looked down on the oil-slicked surface - little rainbows swirled on the dark water and bright green chickweed speckled the edges of the canal.

"I can't hear that dog any more," he said.

The kick that sent the little dog hurtling across the water had the youths howling with glee. One of them even jumped up and down, clapping his hands. It had been a vicious kick, freighted with adolescent venom, which broke several ribs, and left a ragged bundle of fur scrabbling in the canal.

A nice touch would have been if the swans had descended on the mutt in a spitting, hissing rage and beaked it to death but, unsettled by the turn of events, they had swiftly paddled away.

"Here, boy!" one of the youths whispered urgently as the terrier clawed desperately for purchase in the water, its tiny body hunched sideways to favour the stricken bones.

"Here, boy!"

It was heart-wrenching.

"Here, boy! Come here, boy!"

The dog pathetically pummelled its way towards the youth who stretched his arms out towards it.

"Good boy!"

Whimpering and spluttering, its eyes white and terrifyingly huge, the terrier swam towards the boy who reached out, took an ear in each hand, and dragged the dog under water.

A few minutes later, when the last bubble had breached the surface, the boy pulled the dog up, grinned, and released the lifeless form where it drifted on the surface, a matted patch of ragged fur.

"Nice one, James," said the other youth.

Maddox reached into his rucksack and took out a flask. Levering two plastic cups from the top, he took one and poured out a thick, dark coffee and slurped it back. Wiping his mouth with a clean, folded handkerchief, he then re-filled the cup and polished that one off too. When he was finished, he asked Gill if she would like a coffee.

"No thanks."

They both stood up, Maddox hitching up the rucksack over his shoulder; Gill thinking that, actually, she probably wouldn't have minded a coffee after all.

A pied wagtail flitted about in front of them.

"Long-tailed tit," said Maddox.

Seated in the pub, Gill had stopped feeling aggrieved over not being offered a coffee first. She had a nice pint of bitter in front of her, and scampi and chips on its way.

"It's nice here isn't it?" she said.

"Very pleasant. I like the old beams."

"They do a nice pint here," Gill said, taking a generous slurp.

Were they Goths? Maddox wondered at a small gathering of pasty-faced black-clad youngsters sipping their drinks, and looking all pale and existential on the bench in front of them. They were dressed in black or dark greys with spiky hair styles and heavy mascara.

"Tell me about Jonathan Mortimer."

"Jonathan Mortimer? What about him?"

"Well, I haven't met him yet - he's due back on Monday from that residential trip. I'm supposed to be working with him. OK sort of chap is he?"

"He's all right I guess. Just normal."

"Normal?"

"As in 'nothing unusual about him.' He works hard, pleasant manner, quite capable."

"Do you get on with him?"

"Sure - I get on with everyone! Including Sandra although she's probably a lesbian so it's best you don't talk to her - she wouldn't like it."

"I can't imagine you not getting on with anyone," said Maddox with a wolfish grin.

Gill shivered with delight. If she knew what a frisson of heightened sexuality was, she would have shivered with that too.

"But tell me," continued Maddox. "Mortimer - what's he really like?"

"You'll like him. He's very enthusiastic - quite excitable sometimes. He generally keeps himself to himself. Never really goes out - not with people from work anyway."

"Married? Any family?"

"Not that I know of."

"Gay?"

"No, I don't think so. He's got a couple of dogs though."

"Does he have sex with them?"

Gill went full rattle - well throaty, "What are you like! Look, you've made me spill my pint now!"

"Do you think anyone would miss him if he went away?"

"What an odd question - why would you ask me that?"

"No reason."

"Well, I should think he would be missed."

"Would you be missed?"

"I don't think anyone would notice if I just upped and disappeared off the face of the planet!" Gill's rattling laugh filled the pub. It was very much like a death rattle.

CHAPTER THREE

Alice wondered what on earth had possessed her to ask Maddox to tea and, now that he was here, what was she going to do about it?

The fact that it was at her parents house - and not her own flat, didn't exactly help the situation.

Up in her old bedroom, she checked her reflection in the dressing table mirror. Everything was as it should be - ordinary, ordinary Alice. No flaming Titian tresses, no alabaster skin, or eyes like sun-washed emeralds. She'd read in a novel once, of the heroine having 'eyes like black anthracite.'

Hers looked like shit.

As she pulled a brush through her thick black hair, she was outraged to find her hands were trembling slightly and her mouth was dry. She could just do with an ice cream now to calm her down. Most normal people went for Valium, she reached out for vanilla.

This was ridiculous, she didn't fancy Maddox and wasn't sure if she even liked him that much! If truth be told, she had asked Maddox to tea because...well, she didn't know. Was it to prove that she could? Was that why she chose her parents home rather than her own flat - so there would be no suggestion of ulterior motives?

She should be so lucky.

Deep down Alice knew she would have needed far more courage to conjure up a date with the real object of her affections.

The very thought of him punched electric jolts through her body and she knew - just knew to the bones of her body, that Maddox could never provoke such an intensely raw emotion in her and, for that reason alone and for no other, Alice knew she could never love him.

Maddox was never less than polite and courteous. Occasionally he seemed a little distracted, somewhat distant, almost as if he was weighing up the first brush stroke on a blank canvas. However, the general impression was one of basic, down to earth pleasantry - but there was still no room in her heart for anyone other than her 'boyfriend.' She vowed to do something about those inverted commas soon - it was getting silly - her, a thirty-something single woman (thirty-four! - her Inner Voice bleated) mooning over a lad of that tender age. She was almost - almost but not quite - old enough to be his mother. (Yes, you are!)

The doorbell rang and Alice heard her mother clip-clopping down the hallway to open the door - those little steps of hers.

"Hello. Come in. Nice to meet you at last," said Jean holding the door open for Maddox to step through at exactly six o'clock.

At last? Thought Alice, somewhat pissed off. What did her mother mean by at last? It wasn't as if she mentioned his name that much - just said a new colleague had started at the college. She'd suggested tea at the house - her flat was too small. It was the new Assistant Director of the English

27

Language and Literature Department, and Alice didn't want him to think she had ulterior motives.

"You should be so lucky," her mother said.

The family had already had their tea, and Alice and Maddox's meal was set on the table. Cheese and ham cobs, cold beetroot, a small dish of pickled onions, some dips, and stripped celery stalks poking out of a glass tumbler. Crisps and peanuts were splashed into a couple of small dishes. There were chocolate marshmallows and Penguin bars to follow with a hot cup of tea. Maddox asked if he could have coffee instead - he enjoyed tea but always preferred coffee after a meal.

In the back room, Alice could hear Simon and his friend David laughing at something on the television. She wished she was watching with them, on the sofa, and laughing too. On the sofa, laughing with David.

Jean brought the coffee in for Maddox and poured some tea for Alice and herself.

"You can't beat a nice, hot cup of tea," Jean said as she sat down at the table. "Alice tells me you were out walking yesterday."

"Yes - with Gill from the college. We spent the morning walking along the canal, then had a pub lunch."

"They do say Birmingham has more canals than Venice. Isn't that right, Alice?"

"Yes," said Alice, "it's rolled out whenever Birmingham is mentioned on the television or in the newspapers."

Was Gill the real reason that she had asked Maddox to tea - was she simply jealous of Gill going on a walk with him? That was just ridiculous. Maybe it was the ease with which Gill could get on with people that had stoked her envy.

When Maddox had said yes, he would delighted to come to tea and should he bring anything with him, it had thrown Alice into a bit of a tizz. Immediately she had wanted to retract the invitation: ("Oh, did I say come to tea? I meant please don't come to tea!")

It was silly really - no biggie - just tea. No reason for Gill to feel threatened - no cause for her (Alice) to feel guilty or awkward. No point in her parents (them) getting all excited because maybe this is the one for her. The one for their frustrated spinster of a daughter.

"That Gill can be a bit fiery, can't she?" said Jean. "On account of all that red hair and that."

"There is nothing fiery about Gill, Mother, she's a perfectly sweet girl," said Alice, wondering where 'mother' had come from, and not the usual 'mom.' 'Perfectly sweet girl' also was a bit of a mystery, and she found herself cringing at the phrase.

"Alice likes walking, don't you Alice?"

"No."

"Would you like a nice hot cup of tea, Alan?" said Jean, as her husband came into the room. "This is Michael. Michael is Alice's friend from the college. He's a dictator."

"Director."

Alan nodded, shook hands and said he was off to the Horse and Jockey for a pint later, and that they were more than welcome to join him.

"I was there telling Michael that our Alice likes walking, doesn't she Alan?"

"Not really."

Maddox had been an absolute delight. It hadn't taken Alice's mother long to lug out the old Quality Street tin which held all the old photographs of Jean as a girl - Jean as a young lady - Jean.

"This is me up on Barr Beacon feeding the sheep some cheese sandwiches. I wasn't looking when Alan took that one! Just look at the face on me!"

"I can see you were quite a looker in your day, Jean."

No 'Mrs Bullard' - straight into Jean, thought Alice.

There were two large black and white photographs of Jean in a rowing boat.

"This was before I met Alan, of course."

"You don't look a day older," Maddox said.

"Will you listen to yourself," said Jean, squirming with delight.

Jean was a short, squat woman with hardly a neck to speak of. Her grin raced across her face in such a way as to resemble a thing amphibious - a frog or a toad. With her small even teeth barely visible behind an almost lipless mouth, the effect was even more astonishing, and Maddox half expected Jean to lash out a tongue and pluck a moth from the air.

"We are going to the pub!" said Alice.

"But I haven't got the Roses tin down yet."

As they were leaving, Alice glanced in the hallway mirror and checked her reflection. Nothing anthracitey there. Her mother continued to rake through the old photographs; Alice could hear her from the hallway.

"This photo's of Alan and his best friend, Andy, who he's just after meeting at the pub - they were at school together. But look - here's another one of me!"

On Sunday evenings, the Horse and Jockey was quiet. Maddox sat with Alice, across the table from Alan and Alan's best friend, Andy. Alice yawned, she'd been tired all day, and the nervous energy that had been pummelling her throughout seemed to find its mark as the evening wore on.

The pub had once been an old coaching inn, and still sported the ancient oak beams that raced across a low ceiling. Stained and pitted with long-absent woodworm, the old timber looked no less aged than the replica wood burner that smouldered under the mantle, its artificial flame ebb and flowing to a suitably seasonal setting.

"This is nice," Alice said, addressing just Alan and Maddox but ignoring Andy as she had done all evening and before, ever since he rubbed himself up against her when she was a teenager.

30

Alice was just about to mention how tired she was when the doors of the Horse and Jockey swung open, and Simon and David walked through.

"Look what the cat's dragged in," said Alan.

The boys laughed, bought their drinks and pulled up some chairs - they each had a pint of cold lager. Alice looked at her gin and tonic, and thought she might have a lager next. A cold one.

Both Simon and David were in their last year at the Art College. Proper Art College that was - not the flimsy vocational rubbish they ran at Tolkien where any certificate would do so long as you turned up at least half of the time.

David was specialising in Fine Art - his various projects explored and confounded accepted ideals of symmetry where the harmony of the piece challenged you to contradict the absurdity of uncritical elements lying contrary to common perception.

Simon did a bit of drawing.

Alice knew a fair bit about David's projects - it was something to rely on when beginning a conversation. He kept photos of his work on his smart phone, and eagerly sought opinions about them.

"I really like this piece," she once said, when David showed her his latest painting. It looked like apricot jam slammed onto pitted parchment paper and smeared in Marmite.

"It speaks to me."

The South Bank Show was not wasted on Alice.

"It's one of a series," David had said. "I call it Judgment but Not."

"I see," said Alice, not seeing.

"Although maybe I'll just settle on a triptych if I find I can't stretch the sensibilities far enough."

"Wise, very wise," said Alice, not being.

When David had said that it was great that, finally, someone could see what he was striving for, there weren't enough tingles in the world to run up and down her spine.

She was thrilled, she was aglow, and she was seriously in love.

Which was what she wasn't with Maddox, despite half of the college being totally besotted with him. Gill was welcome to him, nice as he was to her, and too good to be true as he was to her mother.

David sipped his pint and turned his head sleepily towards Alice, allowing his copper-coloured eyes to rest on Alice for the slightest of moments, his long lashes giving him the rather beguiling look of a startled antelope.

Simon, in contrast, had the same shit eyes that Alice bore but the slightly slanting edge to his lids made them much more attractive on him than they were on her. Simon took out a cigarette from the packet in his jeans pocket. He grinned at some unheard remark from David to reveal a short rictus of yellow teeth. It was a shame about those teeth, thought Alice who was rather fond of her brother.

Alice was about to ask David how his latest project was going when two thin girls, one dressed in a striped top and tight black leggings - the other girl almost completely smothered in beige - came over and joined them.

"Hello, both," said David. "Glad you could make it."

Alice felt an uncomfortable stirring within her as if she had swallowed a little slippery fish, and it was now thrashing about inside her. Too much eye-shadow, thought Alice, as she smiled at the stripey-top girl and got a sunny "Hi!" in response.

The girl in beige smiled without showing her teeth - even the blusher on her sharp cheekbones seemed the same matching colour. Simon handed her a cigarette, and they both wandered outside to the beer garden while Stripey-top went to the bar.

"I didn't know Simon was seeing anybody," said Alice.

"He's not," said David.

That top looks great on her, thought Alice - and she looks so young and vibrant. She was relieved that the girl's eyes weren't obsidian or anthracite but a tiny nugget of envy ricocheted around inside her, no doubt joining the fish that was still thrashing around in there.

And there within lies the rub, thought Alice when she was sipping on her second lager: Maddox stirred nothing within her but a friend of her brother sent her reeling. It was an infatuation - an unfortunate one - and Alice recognised it as such - even caught herself smiling at the sheer ridiculousness of it all.

She couldn't even remember when she had first met David because there had been no love at first sight - no lust either. David just sort of grew on her and suddenly she found herself thinking about him all the time.

She tried dousing the thoughts, knowing it was never going to happen. She couldn't believe she was willing to barter her own ardour and passion for the remnants of his own friendly, detached affection.

David was much younger than her - she really was almost old enough to be his mother. Comparing him to Maddox was of no use at all. Maddox was good-looking, friendly, ferociously intelligent and rather tall as well - an attractive proposition no matter how you looked at it.

But he wasn't David.

David was laughing at something Stripey-top had said and the little fish swished some. David's laugh was a high-pitched giggle and Alice loved it, even found herself imitating it when he was around.

Seated next to Maddox who was quite easily the best looking man in the whole pub, she yearned to be next to David.

David did have those remarkable long-lashed eyes but there was little else to set him apart. In fact, if his eyes were set a little further apart, he would have been even more appealing. His eyes were a little too close together, and his face was on the chubby side with some budding jowls despite his tender age. Very white teeth in contrast to

Simon's buttermilk gnashers, David also had small, plump and very red lips, with short, spiky brown hair, and clothes of dubious fashion. He was only slightly taller than her too. So all in all, not a great deal to recommend him, but when the requisite parts of the whole were drawn together, she found David irresistible.

But when had it happened - when had that one defining moment occurred when she decided David was the one for her? He was too young, his frame of reference too limited, he was too young, he had little experience of life, he was too young. Alice couldn't quite put her finger on why she felt so uncomfortable thinking the way she did.

Simon and Beige Girl came back in from the garden. Even her shoes were brown (Mary from Reprographics would have suggested taupe). There was some dark stitching around the tops of the shoes, and small elegant bows at the heels. Alice glanced at her own, functional black shoes - like something you would buy from a warehouse.

I need to freshen up my wardrobe, she thought.

"You're very quiet," Maddox said, pulling Alice out of her reverie.

"Sorry - just a bit tired. Been a long day."

"Tell me about yourself."

This was hardly a request. Nor even, Alice thought about it afterwards, a question couched in any terms other than cold, clinical probing - the demand for an answer to a question, as if in a job interview.

"Nothing to tell really."

He had heard already about her degree in Psychology at the University of Birmingham. Although she had completed her teaching qualifications, the prospect of facing a class day after day daunted her to such an extent that she soon found her way into Administration. There also seemed to be considerably less administration in Administration than there was in teaching.

"You must have had boyfriends."

Alice turned away in disdain at the suggestion, it was far too early in their relationship to be discussing such things, not least because the one person she could never discuss was sitting not far away with an attractive young girl lolling over him.

"I don't do relationships," said Alice. "They just strike me as very messy and too wearing. I like being on the shelf."

"You're not on the shelf, a striking woman like you. You certainly don't look forty."

"I'm not, I'm thirty-four!"

She did not want to resent Stripey-top, this young girl who effortlessly, and with no little charm it had to be said, slipped easily into David's sphere - chatting and flirting away, her hands often falling on his shoulder, dropping to his knee.

Gill and Stripey-top - both have made me feel bad about myself lately, Alice sighed.

There were the touchy, feely things going on which marked out a young couple comfortable with each other. Even those recently acquainted could be relied on to dissolve into tactile gainsaying if the chemistry was right.

"Would you mind awfully if I left. I'm really rather tired - it's been a long day," Alice suddenly said to Maddox.

"Of course not. I'll see you tomorrow."

"I rather thought you would be walking me home."

"Would you like me walk you home?"

"Not if you're having a good time here."

"Yes, I'm having a good time here."

"In that case, stay. I'll be fine."

"Are you sure?"

Alice took her leave with a casual wave to everyone, trying hard not to let her eyes rest too long on David who cheerfully acknowledged her with a dazzling smile.

"Nice meeting you," said Stripey-top. The beige girl just smiled - again no teeth.

They could never know Alice's true feelings for David - how could they?

She was almost old enough to be his mother!

CHAPTER FOUR

It had been hell of a job getting the face off him.

But now Maddox wasn't altogether sure if it was worth the effort.

Sitting side by side on the settee, like two recalcitrant lovers, were the life-size latex love doll and the faceless Andy. The rubber doll actually had the face of Andy but it didn't look anything like him which was, by and large, very disappointing.

Must be the lack of connective tissue, thought Maddox, or whatever that stuff was under his face that caused him to prise the face from the skull using a delicate scalpel to snick away at the goo underneath.

Very disappointing. Maddox got up out of the black leather chair and crouched low to appraise his work. He tried to adjust the wet flap of skin on the doll's head but there was just too much give, not enough elasticity.

Faces just weren't robust enough when not attached to the skull.

Maddox strode over to the kitchen and stooped to fish out the steam iron from one of the small fitted cupboards. He plugged it in and twisted the setting to Cotton and Soft Fabrics. A few minutes later, Maddox set about ironing Andy's face to the rubber doll.

It just wouldn't take.

He stepped back and shook his head, decidedly not satisfied with his night's work. Perhaps he should turn the dial up to Linen.

At first, Maddox thought he had punctured the rubber doll despite the care he was taking with the iron but the faint little gurgle he'd heard had, in fact, come from Andy who in the course of the evening had gone from being legless to pretty much off his face.

A tiny bubble of bright blood had popped up on the raw gouge where his mouth had once been, followed by another and another until his lower mandible was dressed in a veritable frogspawn of gore.

Must be arterial, thought Maddox who prided himself on knowing his aortas from his vena cavas. Tenderly he wiped the blood away with a few dabs of tissue before returning to the task at hand.

He had enjoyed the night at the pub. Both Alan and Andy had been good company throughout the evening, and with Alice having already left for home, Maddox slipped effortlessly into their circle.

Andy was a landscape gardener - a good-looking chap with slightly greying hair and thick lips that often split into a wide grin, especially when nudge-nudge-wink-winking about his sexual conquests. Apparently he'd had a mother and daughter once behind the ha-ha that sounded particularly painful to Maddox.

Despite his mature years (Maddox thought late forties/early fifties) Andy could easily carry off the brown leather jacket and blue faded jeans. Alan, by contrast, was dressed head to foot in conservative blue, even down to his pale blue deck shoes. Both had played football for the school team with Andy being something of a star striker and Alan whittling around in defence. Andy still played regularly for the pub team but Alan had long since retired on account of his knees being "fucked!"

"Agony, some mornings," he said.

They had been drinking and playing football for as long as either of them cared to remember, particularly coveting their Friday nights when Alan would often find himself recovering on Andy's sofa, his long limbs scissored in cramped tangles, with crushed empty beer cans littering the floor.

"Does Jean mind?" asked Maddox.

"Who cares," said Alan.

Andy lived in a boxy self-contained flat above a shop, sleeping in a single bed with a purple duvet, and surrounded by pin-ups of scantily-clad girls torn from magazines. Alan would have considered this the fallout debris of a lonely existence, but they had been friends far too long for Alan to ever question Andy's lifestyle choices.

Of course, there had been that business with Alice a good few years ago but Alan had accepted Andy's explanation that he was merely trying to steer her away from the bar with his hips. ("I had me hands full with three Carlsbergs and a Bacardi and Coke!")

Last orders had long been called, and Pat the barman had his arms folded sternly across his chest. Simon and David were going off to some vague nightspot in town with the girls. They claimed their jackets from the pile heaped up on the chair next to Maddox. As they were getting ready to go, Maddox slowly reached back into the pile of jackets and coats, soon finding the pocket he sought.

Outside the pub, Maddox asked if anyone fancied a nightcap back at his - he had a bottle of single malt that wasn't going to drink itself.

"No thanks. I'll be in no shape to tackle Mrs Lavender tomorrow - or her lawn!" said Andy.

Alan was tempted but he had an early start in the morning and had never been able to face whiskey anyway - not since the infamous Johnny Walker incident three years ago.

Zipping up his coat, Andy bade everyone good night and left the pub. If Alice had still been present, she would have ignored him. Alan and Maddox chattered a little while before going their separate ways. As Maddox loitered at the end of the street, it was only a matter of minutes before Andy reappeared.

"I think I left my phone in the pub."

"I wondered who it belonged to," Maddox held up the mobile. "It was jammed down the back of the seat - I wasn't sure whether to leave it with the landlord or not?"

"It's got my entire address book in there - all my contacts," said Andy, taking the mobile and slipping it into his inside jacket pocket. " I don't want to lose it."

"You don't - not with all those addresses in there. Are you sure I can't tempt you with a last nightcap?"

Andy said why not - he wasn't working until the afternoon anyway.

It was nearly midnight when Maddox opened the door to his apartment. Although the room was brightly lit, Maddox walked over towards the settee and switched on the table lamp.

"That's better."

Andy stood in the centre of the room, hovering between the settee and a single black leather chair.

"Please." Maddox indicated the plush leather chair and Andy sat down.

"Nice place."

Maddox opened the door of a small cupboard and took out a bottle of whiskey. He rolled the bottle a couple of times, read the label and nodded his approval.

"Ten years old," he said. "I do like a spot of single malt - can't be doing with all that blended rubbish."

He took a couple of glass tumblers from the same cupboard.

"There's no ice, I'm afraid - but then of course there shouldn't be - not with a good single malt."

Maddox poured a couple of fingers of whiskey into each glass, handed one to Andy, and sat down on the settee.

"I guess we could allow a little water if you wish but the tap water is so tepid here. It doesn't matter how long you run the tap, it never gets cold."

Maddox took off his leather shoes and put on a pair of slippers, which lay beside the chair. Exactly side by side beside the chair.

"I wonder do we have a gardener at the college? I imagine we do - the grounds are quite extensive. I noticed the borders by the gates were turned over this morning, and filled with some sort of mulch or chippings."

"I think the work is contracted out to a company called Crazy Pavings."

"What an unusual name - Crazy Pavings? What do you call your business?"

"Trellis Erections."

"Much better."

Maddox refilled their glasses and placed the bottle next to Andy.

"Help yourself."

After clattering around in the bottom of the fridge, Maddox pulled out a few cans of strong lager and set them on the counter. He then took out a small bottle of tablets from the kitchen cabinet.

"Strong lager is quite acceptable with single malts," he said, handing over a can. "Bitter and mild doesn't really go with some brands but are perfect with malts from the Western Isles."

41

Andy was impressed - Maddox seemed to know so much about so many things.

"What I really like," said Andy, "is women's panties!"

Maddox brought in a small bowl of crackers and some cheese. He took a knife from the drawer and looked at Andy. Then he carefully placed the knife beside the cheese on the board so that it aligned with the edge of the Gouda.

"That looks like a sharp knife," slurred Andy.

"I've put some pizza in the oven," said Maddox as Andy slowly coiled forward in his seat, his arms dangling and swaying from his shoulders as though both wrists had suddenly turned to lead. He pushed himself up and staggered to the toilet, holding onto the back of the chair to steady himself.

Maddox twisted open the bottle of tablets, and dropped several pills into Andy's lager.

Andy soon returned, a few dick splashes staining the front of his faded jeans.

"White panties are the best," he said. "The very best - you can't get better. Trust me, I know."

"Drink up!" Maddox said.

"I really need to get going," he said, looking quite ill and trying hard to focus. "I'm doing Missush Lavender tomorrow."

"Indeed. Well, maybe just a last one for the road then?"

It wasn't long before Andy was unconscious - slumped and canted over the side of the leather chair.

"You hurt me," he slurred when Maddox pinched the nape of his neck.

"Shush."

He wasn't quite ready. Maddox turned on the television and helped himself to a slice of pizza while he watched highlights from Celebrity Scrabble. David Beckham had just got a triple word score on the word 'posh,' which meant the other team forfeited a week's supply of tequila unless the overweight celebrity no-mark on the opposing team could conjure up something with the letters T F C N T A U.

Andy suddenly folded over the cushions, a little dribble lubed out from the corners of his thick, open mouth. Maddox gently propped Andy upright and tickled the back of his neck. No response. He then pinched him quite hard, digging in with his fingernails. Just a grunt. The alcohol and pills seemed to have done the trick.

Maddox put down his pizza and strolled over to the fridge. From the cold tray, he took out a syringe and a small bottle from which he drew up a good slew of Ketamine and jabbed it into Andy.

Andy's eyes flew open.

"Shush now," Maddox reassured the gradually crumpling Andy as he refilled the syringe with more anaesthetic - several infusions would be required over the next couple of hours.

As Andy slumped forward, Maddox finished off his slice of pizza and went back to watching the television.

"It'll be about five minutes," he said to the collapsed Andy, "and then we can begin."

There had been more saliva than Maddox anticipated as he prepared his instruments. He had accepted there would be a fair bit of blood - and that's why he'd bought the smock, which was now arranged around Andy's shoulders with strips of tape holding it tight. Some generous hanks of tissue and kitchen roll were padded down the sides of the leather chair but Maddox hoped they wouldn't be needed if the plastic sheeting did its job.

Having punctured a hole in the deepest point of the jugular groove, Maddox began to drain the blood. Andy wasn't a particularly large man, and there was little fat compressed above the vein. After the initial spurt, there were no great gouts of blood - just a steady flow that Maddox trained into a medley of buckets and saucepans.

As Andy sagged, further injections were administered before Maddox went to work with the scalpel, slicing under the chin and rolling Andy's face away from his skull. There were the usual problem areas - the opening of the nasal passages, always the mouth, and around the eyes but it wasn't long before he was holding a nice, wet circular parchment of skin.

Maddox carefully set the face down on a tray and went to fetch the rubber doll that he had inflated during the commercial break. But despite all the tugging and realigning of the wet flap of skin over the head of the doll, the effect he strove for just wouldn't take. He soon found himself standing before a face-less Andy and a decidedly unsatisfactory piece of work. That would never do for the exhibition.

Perhaps it would be better to collect the limbs and organs first, and leave the face until last after all? But the face seemed the most natural starting point for the project.

Maddox didn't consider his evening a waste - on the contrary it was valuable research. At first, he thought the rubber doll had been an inspired choice but it was obvious he would need something more substantial - a window dresser's mannikin perhaps or some other life-size model. He had seen a model life-size skeleton in the science block during his induction at Tolkien College - perhaps that would have been more appropriate.

A slight whisper and there was another faint expectoration from Andy, a speckle of bubbles blinked around his maw. Most of his hair had been taken off with the scalp but there was a handful or two with which Maddox pulled him up, stretching his throat so he could work it with the knife. And soon Andy was no more.

I'll need to get more whiskey, thought Maddox with a tired sigh. It had been a long night with such little reward at the end. He would take a trip out later in the week before the smell got too ripe - didn't want the neighbours complaining.

Cleaning up as best he could, Maddox grabbed a shower and hoped to squeeze in a couple of hours sleep before the morning.

In the morning, he was meeting his line manager, Jonathan Mortimer, and was looking forward to going over the curriculum for the second semester.

Then he would wait a week or two before texting everyone in Andy's address book:

Gon on hols - Away 4 a while! Girls! Girls! Girls! C U Soon XXX.

CHAPTER FIVE

Jonathan Mortimer, Director of English Language and Literature at Tolkien College, leaned back in his comfortable leather chair, and said with a slight twinge of embarrassment:

"It is not the most demanding of courses to teach on - it's only a level or two up from conventional secondary school standard. We do have a set syllabus that includes twentieth century literature although it only really skates over the big players as it were. There is some Dickens - Great Expectations this year I think - one or two other authors and a little poetry. We had Ted Hughes last year but Seamus Heaney is in line for a recall. Naturally we will use Maya Angelou as an example of how both these disciplines can be incorporated into one work - perhaps Gabriel Garcia Marquez too. We find it easier to start with a bog standard text and gradually introduce the more lyrical elements as they crop up."

"What dinky hands you have," said Maddox.

46

"I'm sorry...?" said Jonathan Mortimer.

He was much younger than Maddox had anticipated - and shorter. Apart from his small hands, the most striking feature about him was his brown eyes, which could be said to have something of the puppy dog about them - and his general clean, scrubbed appearance. In the window behind him, the tight knuckles of Mortimer's spine were reflected running down his starched white shirt. The Director of English Language and Literature was now looking at his hands, and almost but not quite shrugging his shoulders.

"The truth lies in the hands, not in the eyes," said Maddox.

"I beg your pardon?" Mortimer had already expressed incomprehension once, and felt a further apology somewhat in excess.

Splaying out his own long and bony ensemble, Maddox continued, "The hands are the window to the soul. You can learn a lot from hands. There is little evidence of a correlation between lying and eye movements - excessive hand gestures, however, may be a better guide to whether a person is telling the truth."

"I dare say you're right but these," he held up his hands and looked at them quizzically, "do little beyond writing reports, stirring tea and stroking dogs."

"You have a dog?" asked Maddox.

"Two - German Shepherds."

"Now that's what I call a proper dog - none of that toy poodle rubbish. I can't say I'm too keen on those yappy little terriers either."

"Absolutely!" Mortimer's expression bore all the love and admiration for the breed of dog, and it was some time before he got back to the matter at hand.

Maddox closed his eyes and slowly unwound his wide lupine grin as Mortimer outlined his duties and aspirations for the department.

"We do actively encourage the students to write as much as possible," he said, slightly arching his fingers so that the light caught his immaculately buffed cuticles, "but they don't actually need to produce a great deal to get a basic pass. And if they don't pass, we generally put them through anyway rather than refer them back the following year. We want as few of our students repeating these modules as possible."

Maddox tightened his lips. He crossed his legs and, for a moment, cradled his chin in his hand. He then shifted his hand and re-crossed his legs. Eventually deciding that neither attitude suited the impression he wished to convey, he settled back in his chair with an elbow on each arm rest.

Mortimer leaned forward in his chair as if he too was seeking a more desirable stance from which to continue the conversation. He had been leaning back and had momentarily stretched his hands behind his back and, despite the warmth and humidity within the office, there was not so much as a spot of sweat blooming in his pits.

At first impression, Mortimer seemed as cool and starched as his shirts but Maddox had been reassured by a certain fluster to his manner, which occasionally chipped through the calm professional demeanour like a beak through an eggshell. It was a brittle patina that would not withstand Maddox's onslaught over the coming weeks.

"Gill Preston teaches on the creative writing module - she'll acquaint you with the timetable but to be honest, you'll mainly be overseeing the tutorials and literature seminars in the first instance. I imagine it'll be a bit like being in a book club at first."

"Principal Richardson seemed quite keen for me to work on my own," Maddox said. "He seemed to like my critical approach."

At lunchtime, in the staff lounge, Maddox sat in the cheerful room looking at the hyacinths in their earthy terracotta bowls, and munched on a triple sandwich selection. The sandwich had lain face down within his

48

lunchbox, neatly flanked on either side by three cherry tomatoes and a Twix. He liked to start with the prawn sandwich first, and then the ham and mustard, leaving the bacon, lettuce and tomato until last.

"I've had a bugger of a morning," said Gill who had just come in from a bugger of a morning.

She had been smoking outside with Frank from the basement stores, and irritation had added a tousled dimension to her already striking appearance. The tightly-bundled hair was beginning to lose its grip, and her pale complexion sported two fierce red spots. There was hardly an ounce of spare fat on her, and she wore a long grey-speckled jumper scored with tiny pink sequins, cinched in by a thick leather belt.

Gill rattled out a throaty one, then went over to the tiled kitchen area where she unhooked a mug from a line of pegs above the sink. Dashing in a couple of hefty spoonfuls of instant coffee, she strode over to the kettle and filled the mug to the brim.

"No thanks," said Maddox as Gill turned and waved an empty mug at him. She shrugged and walked over to him, clutching the steaming mug in both hands.

"Nice flowers," she said.

"Hyacinths," he offered.

Since their walk along the canal, Gill had seen very little of Maddox who, it has to be said, acted as though nothing else was expected of him.

They had merely strolled along a canal and enjoyed a pub lunch and that was it really. Had she asked him out or had he asked her? She couldn't remember although she'd told Alice that they had sort of asked each other out. It was all so vague. They hadn't kissed, she knew that - not even a little peck.

Gill had greeted the news that Maddox had gone to tea at Alice's with barely a raised eyebrow, despite feeling there should have been a suitable measure of unease at the very least. Nevertheless, she couldn't resist mentioning the walk along the canal again, when they next bumped into each other along the corridor.

"We walked for miles," said Gill.

"We went to the pub," countered Alice. "We stayed all night and had a great time."

That was it really - no locking of horns, no hackles raised. There was something about Maddox - and that was a phrase that seemed to echo throughout the college - which didn't invite possession or ownership. He possessed a certain quality that suggested all intimacy was by rote only, an over-indulgence rarely ventured into or given permission for.

But even now, Gill recalled the strange detachment of Maddox when he had given her a lift back to the train station after their day out. It still irked her a little.

"You could have dropped me off at my house if it was a bit closer," she had said.

"Yes, I could have," he had replied before sweeping out of the station car park to leave Gill trailing a forlorn finger down the train timetables.

Later in the week, Maddox suggested to Gill that they should think about going to the Lake District for a weekend.

"I love the Lakes!" said Gill, who hated the Lakes.

Perhaps she was in competition with Alice after all because she suddenly found herself yearning to mention it. She made her way to the main office.

"I thought you couldn't stand the Lake District," Alice said.

"No - I just hate the touristy parts. You know - Windermere, Dove Cottage, that Beatrix Potter house."

"You said the Lakes could go fuck itself. You said it was a dreary trumped-up honey pot sucking in pikey arseholes from the suburbs."

"What I meant," said Gill with more than a suggestion of huff, "was the tweeness of it all - the daffodils, the dry stone walling - those tiny little humpback bridges squished up like stone accordions. (She was going to use that one in her creative writing classes). I dare say Michael and I will be straddling Great Cock-up."

"Well, you should have a lovely time if you get the weather," said Alice sweetly.

What she really wanted to say was "Whatever!" She loved saying that. She'd often heard David saying it with such effect. One of the office girls had said it once, and it didn't sound half as good. Such a curt little throwaway line that carried bundles of weight.

She found herself thinking of David again. Of his bright, white smile and the way his eyes crinkled as his face split into a grin. She had noticed that he had a little mole tucked just under his chin along the line of his jaw, and that his eyelashes weren't as curly as she'd first thought but slanted slightly downwards.

Gill was still gabbling on, comparing the Cumbrian scenery with the rugged Atlas Mountains of Morocco and the noticeable lack of twee amongst the Berbers.

"I'm sure you're right. I wouldn't know," said Alice, turning back to her computer keyboard and tapping an end to the conversation.

Jonathan Mortimer had crumbled before Maddox. Rarely had he met anyone with such forceful charisma although, admittedly, he did need to get out more often.

It was not long before Maddox felt he owned a bright, companionable dog rather than a line manager and had half-expected Mortimer at any minute to roll over and have his tummy tickled.

"You must play the piano or mend Swiss watches with hands like those. They really are most expressive. Perhaps, Jon, you build model ships out of matchsticks."

"Not at all," said Mortimer.

"Then you must write or paint. Those are painterly hands."

"Well as a matter of fact, I've a few jottings put to one side which I intend to pull together one day."

"Yes, it is obvious - with hands like those."

Jonathan Mortimer held up his hands, turning them slowly and nodding his head, as if it had been obvious from the start.

"You strike me," said Mortimer, "as being a very perceptive man."

"I am, Jonny - very perceptive - and it is to your credit that not only do you recognise this but are also prepared to give me free reign over the syllabus as I see fit."

"It would go without saying."

"Of course it would."

Jonathan Mortimer appraised his hands some more. They were certainly on the small side, with the index and ring fingers spanning the exact same length.

"It may be useful to have a word about recent absenteeism which has increased since last year. In fact, there was a thirteen per cent increase to be precise. I'm mentioning this statistic only because Principal Richardson keeps badgering me about it."

"Any ideas?"

"As to why the absenteeism? No, not really - it's not as if the students are forced onto these courses. It's not school or kindergarten. They only have to attend eighty per cent of the time to qualify for a pass anyway."

"So, in effect, they would only have to turn up four days out of five then?"

"As good as - I don't know what half of the students are doing on some of the courses. You should see the students on Early Childhood Learning. You wouldn't put one of those in charge of a goldfish never mind your child."

Mortimer's puppy-dog eyes suddenly blinked rapidly, little skin shutters shuffling like poker cards, almost as if he was coming out of a trance. Perhaps he felt such candidness inappropriate to a new member of staff, and was not in keeping with his senior position.

"I'll discuss it with the lecturers and see what we can come up with. Anything else I might need to know?"

It was startling this effect that the new man had on him. If he hadn't gone so puppyish, its possible he may just have detected the faintest trace of interest with which Maddox asked:

"Any problem students?"

But such was the measured delivery of Maddox's enquiry, it was unlikely such probing would have been picked up as anything more than professional curiosity.

"No, none to speak of really. There are a couple of lads in the creative writing group who are repeating this year - James Jones and Hawthorn Smethwick. Not bad lads really - just easily distracted. This is their second year of repeating the module so they'll be a bit older than the new intake, not that it makes any difference."

"Easily distracted, you say?"

"Sorry?"

"Easily distracted?"

"Yes, sorry, miles away."

"I'll see what I can do."

A slight smile tugged the corners of Maddox's thin mouth as he stood up and left the office.

Alice had received her first text message from David. It said: CHEERS ALICE!

She had asked Simon and David if they'd be interested in seeing a contemporary art exhibition that was being held in the city centre.

"No chance," said Simon.

"Might be worth a look," said David.

Pretty much the responses Alice would have expected - and hoped for.

She had read about it in the local paper - an installation by an eighty-nine year old Serbian, which involved a row of birdcages with tins of sardines in them. If David was interested, she would (oh, but she could be so casual) text him the details. (If I could just get your mobile number...)

Alice was sat at her desk and, without lifting her eyes from her mobile, said to Val, "Oh, it's a text from this lad who's quite sweet on me."

Sweet on me! Jeez - it's like something out of Pride and Prejudice, I'll have him in riding breeches and a wet shirt next, she thought. The image, fleeting as it was, derailed any further thought. She would add a crop later on when she thought about him before falling asleep.

UR WELCUM DAVE! She replied and waited for his response. Would he reply? Was it necessary to reply to her text? Did she leave it open-ended enough? Should she have put a kiss - a big X at the end of her text? She took care not to delete the message and saved it into her archive. She placed the mobile next to her keyboard so she could feel the vibration if he responded. There was no hanging on the telephone these days - it was all about trilling text alerts.

"I thought it might be from Michael Maddox," said Val.

Val was, like many who had met him, quite taken with Maddox. She had also enjoyed the simmering waspish exchanges between Alice and Gill despite thinking it a pity that she wasn't being cited as someone Maddox had taken out on a walk or had tea with. Val would often head to the washrooms after seeing Maddox in case she had something stuck in her teeth or a dab of relish smudged on one of her chins. I don't make enough of myself, she said to herself. Her bright blue eyes were no longer deep-set and beguiling but were already sinking in the fleshy mounds of her face.

"Mr Maddox is of no concern of mine," said Alice.

"He's definitely got something though."

"Got something, all right," piped up Sandra who had him in her sights soon as she'd done with Ross. She blew out her cheeks and puffed out her chest causing a nose-ring to invert, and the tattoo on her left breast to balloon out.

"I know someone who's been getting a bit of that," sniggered Sandra, looking over as Gill sauntered into the office.

I've not been getting any of that, thought Gill - not even a bit of it.

"He's got a bit of an evil grin wouldn't you say?" said Jackie. "He's very well qualified but it didn't say on his application form whether he was single or not. Or his age come to that."

"My mother really likes him," said Alice, "and I think my father likes him too. They went to the pub at the weekend. In fact, we all did."

Val stopped typing and sent her document to print. She wobbled over to collect it, tutted and returned to her computer, made a small correction and sent it to print again. Her large face, pinked and set, remained expressionless, unsure whether or not to contribute to the conversation. Any further talk and banter seemed somewhat irreverent even though Maddox was coming out of it rather well.

"I think everyone likes him, but Frank can't stand him," continued Sandra, looking out over her stacked in-tray.

"Who?"

"Frank from the basement stores - you know, that mardy so and so who's always moaning about doing the job he's paid to do. He calls Maddox the Grinning Assassin."

"How would Frank know, for goodness sake!"

"He says he can tell. It's in the eyes."

"He's got lovely eyes has Mr Maddox. All treacly and brown," said Val, finally mustering up a comment.

"I'd say hazel."

Mary, from Art & Design, would have assured them that they were green.

"I don't like Frank - never have," Sandra said, managing to

make his name sound snide. Ross had told her about the teasing he gets from Frank each Monday morning when he turns up for work with a new batch of love bites.

"Good afternoon, everyone."

There was a collective coo as Maddox suddenly entered the office, holding a bunch of files. He was wearing one of his dark tailored suits with a pale yellow shirt and tiny silver cuff links. Alice couldn't think of anyone else who wore cuff links. Sandra quickly realigned her nose-ring.

Maddox walked over to Alice's desk who, despite herself, rather enjoyed the attention.

She quickly glanced down at her mobile - there had been no incoming message, no flash of text - no trembling vibration. Not from her phone anyway. Sliding the lock across on the mobile, she dropped it into her handbag. David probably had his phone switched off. She might text him again later on in case he hadn't received that last text.

"I just wanted to thank you again for tea. It was splendid," said Maddox.

"You're welcome. Mother was certainly taken with you. Did you stay long at the pub?"

"Not too long - I had to get back. I had some ironing to do."

CHAPTER SIX

"I'm guessing," said David, "that the installations are experimental, aimed at provoking the viewer into reflecting upon their own processes of interpretation, and the discrepancy between assumed knowledge and that, which is produced through actual experience."

"Eh?" said Alice.

"Although that's not to say there isn't a definite theme running through the work - it is fairly obvious when you look at it."

"Eh?" said Alice again.

They stood facing a row of gilded birdcages, each one harbouring a tin of sardines. There seemed to be mathematical precisions in the arrangement with each cage on its own stand matched up to a chalked marker on the floor.

Alice scrunched up her face in what she hoped reflected intense absorption.

"Do you think," Alice began, perhaps unsure about the question she was about to pose. "Do you think there's any reason why one cage has got sardines in sunflower oil and some of the others have tomato?"

"Perhaps," David shrugged, "it's meant to challenge our perception of continuity."

A pause.

"Its just a load of bollocks really, isn't it?" said Alice.

David's face broke into a wide grin and Alice loved him even more for it, his surprisingly red lips stretched into the most devastating of smiles. If only she could face that first flush of joy every waking moment of her day. You wouldn't ever think such a tender mouth could hold what they did - two wide white rows of gleaming teeth, the lower jaw seeming to ever-so-slightly jut out a fraction whenever he laughed or smiled which was often.

His breath was pure mint and Alice wondered if he would taste sour in the mornings. She longed to find out - his were proper rosebud lips, as if rendered by a Pre-Raphaelite artist, with the painterly curves and downstrokes of an expert brush. It was then that she resolved - promised herself fervently - that one day those lips would be clamped to hers, and she would taste him. Sweet or sour, fresh spring grass or turned milk - she would have his breath.

How at ease she felt in his company given the weeks, months (surely not a year!) she had spent thinking about him. Here in this little art gallery, she was with him or, rather - he was here with her. It was his choice, a choice he had made - to be here right now - with her.

"I thought you were into all this?" Alice said, gesturing at the fishy cages.

"Installations are not really my thing," he said, stepping back as if to peruse the collection more objectively.

There were other people in the gallery, transfixed in varying degrees of absorption or consternation. Had it been a mistake asking him to come here? Such was his disparagement that Alice wondered if she may become tainted by association - the girl who thought he liked trash.

David was slightly taller than Alice but only a tad. When they had been looking at the garish paintings in the lower galleries, all multi-coloured swirls and eddies, it had been enough for her to lean imperceptibly into him and smell his scent. Alice had held her breath and took in a short sharp sniff. There was a slight acrid buzz coming off him, but she soon drew in the smell of his thick, slightly spiked mousey hair and thought she could also detect an exotic fragrance.

"Do you want to get a drink?" he said.

More than everything in this whole world did Alice want to get a drink.

The day was just getting better and better for Alice. The bus had been on time, and a short walk took her to the gallery through paved open squares and trim-bricked corridors. Alice clipped along the pavement, throwing her head back as though trying to shake off an irksome scarf.

The gallery itself had been converted from an old neo-gothic school. Tastefully lit with sandstone walls, it could have been stone-cladded as far as Alice was concerned.

Before meeting David, she had been sucking on an ice-lolly and had gnawed off the last slivers of red ice from the stick and dropped it in a bin. She checked her lips for rogue candy sprinkles in a small compact mirror.

David had been waiting just inside the gallery foyer (he was waiting for her!) and even as he slouched against the wall, he did so with a languid feline grace. With jeans just about clinging to his hips, and an incongruous green silk scarf pulled taut to his neck, Alice thought that he looked like a work of art himself.

They were soon sitting opposite each other in the gallery cafe, a bright, airy enclave that tiptoed outside onto a mica-shot patio with low jaggy shrubs. They both had Cappuccinos even though Alice wasn't keen and usually took her coffee with the barest threat of milk. Hunched over their drinks, Alice imagined the scenario - a young mother and her son? Alice was immediately furious with herself, refusing to countenance such thinking any further. David was younger than her - big deal! It wasn't as if there was a yawning abyss.

David pecked at his Cappuccino.

"Lovely!" he said.

"So, you weren't keen then?" Alice's voice was devoid of anxiety despite wanting to distance herself from any culpability. But she was good at composure - or, at least, thought she was - and her feigned nonchalance struck just the right balance.

"Oh, don't get me wrong," he said. "I enjoyed the exhibition - it was certainly useful. I have to cite several references for my final year project and an obscure artist from some scattered village in the distant foothills of Serbia will have my tutors drooling."

David had an unusually high timbre to his voice whenever he was excited, and Alice was pleased to see it register when he was with her.

"It's just that I find installations such a cop out," he said, suddenly mustering a pout of disdain.

"It says here in this brochure," Alice flapped open a pamphlet and threw her hair back with an unnecessary flourish, "that 'the artist's work seeks to occupy a space that, by filling it, creates an opposite void that generates the energy in the first place.'"

"That's just the sort of guff I write that gets me Merits and Distinctions and a pat on the head for virtually every single piece of work I do at the college."

Alice, for the third time that morning, could feel another Eh? coming on.

"It's a classic cop out - all you have to do is justify anything and everything you do. It's all in the sales pitch - you don't even need to be able to draw or paint to get a degree in art - it's standard practice!"

"But Simon said you were good."

"I am good but Simon's better - much better. He can sketch and draw and paint just about anything but because they all look like the thing he's drawing, he never gets marked up. I get higher marks purely because I bullshit better than he does."

Some of the froth from David's Cappuccino snagged on his upper lip and he flicked it off with his tongue and then dabbed at his mouth with a paper napkin. Alice saw where the besmirched napkin was casually scrunched up, and left to one side of his saucer.

"It's all about the right words really," David continued, and Alice felt it was an opinion that he had probably aired on many occasions. "Especially words like 'challenge' and 'interrogate' and 'contradict.' Just mix them up, add a sprinkling of pretension, and the lecturers will have orgasms over it."

David and orgasms were two words that went together very well for Alice who was always on the look-out for more material for her day-dreaming montages.

"If you challenge the viewer to interrogate a painting, and to put their own interpretations on the contradictions within the piece - you're onto a winner!" said David and Alice laughed (a little too loudly) as if she had been let in on a great secret.

She'd kept all his text messages. It pained her to delete the messages but she eventually struck on recording them in her diary. She even kept the form they were sent in, all the spelling mistakes, the abbreviated fragments of wording, the abrupt capital letters, the single uses of the word 'yes' and the over used exclamation marks. Now she was coveting a balled-up napkin that was possibly smeared with his saliva. How had it got so bad?

Not far from the art gallery, in one of the brass and chrome bars on Broad Street, Gill also had saliva on the mind.

"Those little shits! I wouldn't spit on them if they were on fire!"

"I gather you are referring to the two James's?"

"They are doing my head in!"

Maddox had only heard about the two James's - he had yet to meet them, and he was quite looking forward to the experience. You could see that Gill's head had been done in when she met Maddox inside the pub - the mildest of irritations always brought weals of colour to her cheeks.

"I thought you'd be waiting outside for me," she said at first.

"Did you?" said Maddox.

Maddox paid for the drinks and they made their way to one of the tables. He watched with curious intent as Gill sat down across from him - she seemed to collapse in her seat, the layers of woolly jumpers, scarfs and fleeces more of a trailing entourage than mere clothing.

"I'm gonna have the biggest burger on the menu," she waved a laminated menu at him. "With chips."

As they faced each other across the small fixed table, their knees couldn't help but bump against each other.

"It's not that they're that bad - just bloody annoying really," said Gill. "Although there is a really spiteful side to them. Maybe I should just ignore them - chill out a bit."

"That would seem to be the best approach."

"But it doesn't seem fair on the other students."

"Life isn't fair. It's a good learning curve for the rest of them."

Maddox sat easily in his chair, plucking at a beer-mat with his long, bony fingers and looking up at the low-ceiling. A tea-coloured water stain peeled away into the corner; the windows by the door were small and cobbled, curtained by the long bleached drapes that hung on either side of them. Maddox looked at Gill again, this time with half-closed, detached and studious eyes. She was glancing at the menu, checking out the side orders, and the low light accentuated

62

her features with a softness that interested - or rather alerted Maddox to certain possibilities.

In the subdued lighting, Gill's pale complexion and low features, framed as they were with masses of red, corkscrewing hair, produced no dramatic planes and sharp angles but rather offered up a delicate blend of creamy tones.

"Perhaps I can take your class for a couple of weeks?" he said.

Gill pushed a few stray twists of hair back off her face, and Maddox noticed her ears were larger than he would have liked.

"No, it's OK," she sighed. "It won't be for long anyway."

Maddox leaned back further into his chair, "Are you still thinking of taking a career break next year?"

"I think so - maybe Brazil, although I've heard the Bolivians are very hospitable."

Gill decided on extra cheese and bacon with a side order of onion rings.

"You'll never guess what they were doing today."

"Who - the Bolivians?"

"No, the two James's - they were throwing Maltesers at one of the students - that big girl with the Afro - apparently they were going for a new record. Can you imagine - sixteen Maltesers stuck in that poor girl's hair!"

David's mobile flashed several times with incoming text messages as they sat sipping their drinks. He would quickly read them, smile, and punch out a reply with a speed that left Alice agog with even more admiration.

"Someone after you?" she said, desperately hoping there wasn't.

"No one in particular," he replied.

Alice smiled as though she wasn't particularly bothered. "You know," she said, "I've really enjoyed today - it was different."

"So have I - thanks for coming."

Thanks for coming! He was appreciative of her company - he could as easily have not said anything. Alice took a sip of her coffee and slowly tapped the table with her fingers.

"I was just thinking," she began, "maybe we could..."

David's mobile rang this time, a shrill ringtone - a tune she recognised but couldn't place. He got up and shuffled around the table in that appealing louche manner of his, the mobile phone pinned to his ear.

Although she was looking up at him with a fixed smile that was desperately trying not to turn into a grimace, David turned away and took the call further away from the table. Alice looked into her coffee, as if her future could be divined from the frothy dregs that clung to the porcelain.

"I have to go now," he said, folding the mobile back into his back pocket. "It's Simon - I'm meeting him at the Arcadian."

The Arcadian - where all the young people go.

"Come along if you like?"

"No, it's OK,' she said, pulling her bag from out under the table and hoisting it onto a shoulder. "I'd best be off - things to do."

"OK, see you later. Bye Alice."

Her name was the last thing on his lips as he left. Alice watched him go but he didn't melt into the crowd. He sauntered through the square, hands in pockets, before lightly turning and walking out of sight.

In her hand, she clutched a soiled napkin.

CHAPTER SEVEN

His leather shoes stepped across the tight woven loops of
the carpet, a trim square of turquoise and grey laid down in
the exact mid-centre of the hallway. Just inside the hall, a
pair of antique Chinese vases stood either side of the
doorway, and some roughly-hewn ebony statuettes were
perched on a rosewood bureau. It was the briefest of
observations for Maddox's interest lay elsewhere.

There were only two possessions he truly coveted - they
came in a pair, and unfortunately hung off the end of
Mortimer's wrists. It had been a while since he had seen
such perfect hands, and he wanted them.

"Thanks for coming," said Mortimer, holding up two large
glasses of red wine in those very hands.

"Thanks for inviting me," said Maddox, taking one of the
glasses. "I gather you wanted to discuss the team building
event for next year?"

"Plenty of time for that," he gestured for Maddox to go
through to the lounge.

Maddox had readily accepted the invitation - there was a
DVD that Mortimer was keen to get some feedback on -
something relevant to the team building exercise.

Or I could just borrow the DVD? Maddox had almost replied but opportunity cannot afford to be relinquished so easily, and he agreed to come over that very evening.

In one of the Chinese vases there were some flowers - chrysanthemums quite possibly, and so finely petaled, he was sure that if he touched them they would crumble and fall to the floor.

The house was warm, the central heating on high, and everything seemed hot to Maddox. His eyes quickly scanned the room. Tall earthenware urns spouted exotic orchids, and plump cacti peeked sullenly over rims of tiny terracotta pots. Batiks hung from one wall next to unframed canvases - burnt driftwood lay upon a cabinet next to marbled conch shells.

Maddox was drawn to the array of spears that crisscrossed the panelling of one wall.

"The assegai," said Maddox, who knew a piercing weapon when he saw one. "The famous stabbing spear favoured by the Zulu nation, I believe."

"Correct - I often wonder if any of mine were ever used to kill anybody."

In stark contrast, the adjoining room was floored with blonde hardwood and furnished in leather - washable leather. Polished porcelain ornaments, shiny-new as if straight from their boxes, lined the mantel with a chessboard precision. In fact, in a corner of the room, there was a chessboard lined up in the exact centre of a small table with bevelled edges and chrome legs, it's pieces fashioned in glass and each pawn, bishop and knight arranged perfectly on their squares.

"Take a seat," said Mortimer. "Sorry about the clutter - there are some things I just can't help collecting."

"Very eclectic," said Maddox, thinking perhaps a favourable opinion was expected of him.

Mortimer beamed and took a sip of his wine, slowly chuntering it through his teeth before swallowing.

"I got apricots with that one, and just a hint of smoked loganberry," he said.

Maddox gently sniffed at his wine but could only detect the faint whiff of the dogs that Gill had mentioned.

Such was the attention Mortimer was paying him, even his suddenly flaring nostrils drew an apologetic response.

"Sorry about the smell, that'll be the dogs - they're not actually allowed in these rooms but their smell does tend to creep in a little," Mortimer whispered conspiratorially as if he was about to betray a confidence. "Perhaps you would like to meet the dogs?"

The dogs were hunkered down in a pen of their own, behind a low screen of galvanised steel that partitioned part of the large kitchen. The kitchen was surprisingly messy with opened tins of dog food and spilled biscuits.

The dogs rose slowly to their feet and padded over to them, claws clicking like metronomes on the stained and sticky linoleum floor. They were fierce, bedraggled creatures with staring coats and baleful yellow eyes that looked loose in their sockets. Both animals fixed hateful eyes on Maddox but such was the malevolence with which he returned their stare they both shrank back.

Maddox smiled, "How sweet - Alsatians."

"Not Alsatians - German Shepherds. It was only during the war they were called Alsatians - anything 'German' was considered inappropriate," said Mortimer.

"Inappropriate, indeed."

As Mortimer bent down to ruffle the dogs, Maddox slipped silently back into the lounge, and consulted the vast array of spears along the wall. Lifting one of the assegais from its mooring, he approved of the heft of the weapon as he curled his long, bony fingers around the shaft.

"Who's been a good boy then?" Mortimer gushed at the larger of the dogs, as he leaned over the screen and vigorously shook the animal's head so it became almost a blur, and quite possibly unhinged its eyes even further.

Maddox slipped back into the kitchen, holding the short, stabbing spear.

Bent as he was over the dog, Mortimer's shirt was pulled tight across his back, stretched taut as a white ripe fruit about to burst. Still no sweat or lint marked the immaculate shirt, and Maddox did not feel inclined to pop that illusion of pristine vanilla freshness with hot beads of ruby red.

Instead, he considered Mortimer's buttocks. Braced as he was with his weight firmly on the balls of his feet, Mortimer presented his arse as a perfect target that could soon, if Maddox had a mind to, be bristling with more stabbing spears than those that lined the walls.

He looked down at the spear he had chosen. It was a beautiful weapon that he had in his hand, with an irresistible target presenting itself. Mortimer had his back turned to him, bent over and giddily fussing over the dogs.

Maddox relaxed his grip on the assegai, allowing the spear to gently roll in the palm of his hand. Maddox caressed the shaft with his long fingers, and ticked his arm back and forth in a slow pendulous fashion.

"Now Binky, what are you doing skulking there at the back?"

The encouraging words brought the other dog over to him, which duly rolled over to present a tummy in need of a tickle. Mortimer stretched further over the screen to rub the dog, which barked and wagged with undisguised pleasure, its hot paws pedalling the air.

Like the legs of a primeval jointed creature, Maddox's fingers curled around the shaft of the spear and clenched it tightly. Drawing the spear back, he stepped back, bracing all his weight on the one foot. The ridges of his calves surfaced like tiny breaking fish, and he could feel his shoulders lock as he tightened his grip on the spear.

"You are a silly-billy - coming over all shy and unnecessary just because we have a visitor."

The dog responded to Mortimer's gentle chiding by sitting

up and thrumming its tail on the clacky linoleum floor; it soon rolled over to have its tummy rubbed again. As Mortimer obliged by leaning further over the screen, he rose up on the tips of his toes to present his chino-clad buttocks in all their wriggling glory.

"Who's a silly billy? Yes you are - yes you are..."

Alice was in a quandary.

Maddox was the obvious choice if it came to potential partner material - stable, polite, good job - great prospects (everyone at Tolkien said so). Everyone it seemed, her mother included, was in his absolute thrall. Alice knew her mother would be delighted beyond belief if her only daughter (quiet-shy-but-somewhat-headstrong-with-self-deprecating-tendencies - Alice knew her Cosmopolitan personality types) started dating him.

But he didn't make her tingle. Unlike David.

Was there a single scenario she hadn't played out in her mind? So many scenelets had fluttered idiotically through her mind lately. Including the agonising tableaux where David announces his impending marriage to another girl. Of course, Alice would gush good luck and underplay the response. In a bizarre, unsettling way, Alice thought she might even welcome the sense of martyrdom such as it would be - the delicious bereavement of a loss that she had never owned in the first place.

Of course, she would be crushed at first. Her stomach would heave but her ever-reliable sensibility and formidable powers of recovery would prop her up. She would be able to say how wonderful and how marvellous and how absolutely super it all was while inside she would scream and writhe. This was where Alice always felt short-changed by her own lack of selfish accountability. How was he ever to know her true feelings if she kept them concealed and boxed away?

She did not love Maddox. She was positive she didn't fancy

him, and yet she was curiously drawn to him. Was it because he was coveted by just about everyone else that made him so desirable? How sure was she that she didn't fancy him anyway - did there have to be a spark or a dramatic, violent surge on the electricity grid? Maddox was certainly well-dressed and well-spoken and well-everything - his charming manner and formidable mind were undeniably attractive.

Was this obsession with David getting in the way of truer feelings for Maddox? Although not particularly muscular, Maddox was lean and taut - he dressed with a taste for classic lines, which was more than could be said of David whose pot-holed jeans barely clung to his hip bones.

The day that Maddox had joined Alice for tea, it was as if a celebrity had sat down in the midst of them. Her mother had even lamented the fact afterwards that she had bought sliced ham from Tesco, and not off-the-bone from Clinton's Butchers on the High Street.

But on the rare occasions that she pictured herself as a potential Mrs Maddox (with punnets of freshly-picked strawberries from the garden, and plumped-up scatter cushions in the lounge), always looming into view would be David.

David, David, David. It didn't trip off her tongue. She relished the enunciation and let the syllables slurp off her tongue. Now that was surely love, and she could almost sense the little shiver of stars spangling around her.

Despite all this, her imagination refused to serve up punnets and soft furnishings with David. Instead it presented a tableau of the short and the sweet that never dared to venture beyond the immediate present. Perhaps one moment, one fleeting treasured moment with David would be enough - sufficient to staunch any further longing so that she could get back to her life, living her life - enjoying a life without the merest mention of his name.

Jonathan Mortimer had felt some pain in his time but nothing like this. His eyes had flown so wide open in a gasp of sheer agony that they threatened to explode out of their sockets. His teeth bit down in an enamel-cracking grimace that opened up into a spluttering howl and, such was the shrill piercing cry that followed, the startled Binky quickly released his teeth from Mortimer's hand and scrambled backwards.

"That is so sore - and so uncalled for!" Mortimer's eyes pooled with tears as he clutched the bleeding hand to his chest. He then held it away from his shirt, quickly moving towards the sink as the first drops of blood began to spatter the floor.

There were some unwashed pots and a frying pan to get through but Mortimer nudged them aside with his elbow before turning the cold water tap on.

Maddox was astonished - not only by the unprovoked attack by the dog, which was remarkable in itself, but by the sheer facility of Jonathan Mortimer's elbows as he had somehow contrived to dig a space through the pots and pans, and turn on the tap without once seeming to use his hands. It was no wonder they were the most beautiful hands he had ever seen - they were hardly ever used.

"Allow me." Maddox placed the assegai down on the table before flapping open a clean dishcloth and handing it to Mortimer. "It looks quite nasty."

"Thank you - I don't know what came over him. He's not normally so vicious."

"Not normally?"

"No, usually he's quite placid but sometimes he gets one on him." Mortimer wrapped the tea towel tightly around his injured hand. "Perhaps he was feeling a bit jealous."

Maddox turned to face the dogs and they instinctively backed away, their claws skittering on the cold linoleum. Not even a growl crawled out of their throats but their hackles bloomed like molehills on a prize lawn. Both

71

animals padded backwards and cowered in the furthest corner of the pen.

Pink water swirled around the sink as Mortimer rinsed the cloth and wrapped it around his bitten hand.

No use to me now, thought Maddox. He needed a pristine pair without indents. The elbows could be an alternative - they were versatile but hardly comely.

"Hold your arm up," he told Mortimer. "It may help to stem the flow."

Maddox glared at the dogs, which began to whimper - a low tapering whine. He looked at their low-slung bellies and sharp, biting teeth and wondered if they may be of some use to him. He decided they would.

Alice knew that it wouldn't be long before she grew bored with David.

It would only be natural. They had nothing in common for a start and, reluctant pragmatist that she was, Alice knew it was extremely unlikely that David felt the same way about her as she did about him.

She tried hard to imagine a future with David and couldn't get past a frosted vignette of the two of them walking in a wild flower meadow.

She'd be wearing a pale yellow summer dress; he would be dressed in white linen trousers with a blue jumper thrown loosely over a shoulder. They would be laughing - then it all stops as if the whole scenario was so ridiculous that her imagination sensors must have shut down - the little synapses refusing to snap such ludicrous imagery across their network.

All she can deal with is a present where there is a David who, partial to a drink as she was sure he was (weren't all students partial to a drink?) might possibly succumb to a drunken fumble one night. But it all seemed so predatory and unseemly, and Alice soon felt another sigh coming on.

Jonathan Mortimer's hand was wrapped tightly in a bright white crepe bandage and secured with a safety pin and tape; tiny pink spots of blood flowered through the gauze. Maddox was surprised that the elbows hadn't been used to clip the pin into place but remained impressed by the dexterity of those hands nevertheless.

"I was right about the hands," Maddox said.

They were sitting on either end of the long leather sofa watching the television. A wildlife documentary was showing with the sound turned down. Some lionesses were advancing on a zebra.

"You will probably need a tetanus shot," said Maddox.

He continued to look around the room. There was a coat-stand in one corner of the room. Two coats hung from the pegs - one a black leather jacket, and the other Herringbone Tweed with leather buttons. Maddox was sure that if he was to put his hand into the silk lining of the Tweed's pockets, there would be nothing in there, no lint, no mints - just an exquisitely beaded seam. The colour of the jacket was a mixture of brown with barely discernible orange flecks.

The lionesses had brought down the zebra and were now tearing into it. The zebra's hooves flailed uselessly in the dust, and a close up showed some carnassial teeth shearing through a striped shoulder.

"I'll put the DVD on in a minute," Mortimer said.

Maddox wasn't keen on brown, and orange wouldn't be his first choice either, but the tweed seemed just about right for Mortimer.

I wouldn't expect anything less, Maddox thought with an approving smile. Mortimer had impressed him with his meticulous tastes, innate fastidiousness and analytical mind. He was genuinely pleased that he had spared him - the world needs more sophisticates. At least, for now, it has retained another.

There would always be time for the mangled paw to heal itself.

Mortimer slid the DVD into the drive, and Maddox took a sip of wine as the opening credits flashed up on the screen: Developing Minds - Team Building and Motivation in the Wilderness.

"I hope there's no blood," said Maddox.

CHAPTER EIGHT

"No, I don't think he ever had a girlfriend," Alan said, looking across at the police officers, and trying hard not to sound apologetic. "In fact, I'm pretty sure he didn't."

"But he was always going on about girls," said Jean.

Police Inspector Archie Lively sighed, his voice laden with professional tedium.

"No known partner."

He jotted it down in his little black book.

Jean huddled on a chair, her hands clasped together on the kitchen table, feet tapping away on the lino.

"Would you like a nice hot cup of tea, sergeants?" Jean only knew of constables and sergeants, and wasn't going to waste time addressing the policemen as anything less than sergeants.

"Lovely," said PC Walduck.

"There's no fault or blame attached to Mr Andrew White having gone missing," said Inspector Lively. "We're just following up on the initial report, which is routine procedure in such circumstances."

He consulted his little book.

"And you say his last known whereabouts were...?"

"The Horse and Jockey - the pub just down the road - but I'm sure he left before us. He had an early start in the morning."

Inspector Lively was a tired-looking, short-haired man, grounded in middle age, with close-set eyes and a significantly upturned, somewhat nostrilly nose - not the best of features for a policeman.

Though younger, PC Walduck was about the same size as his colleague but smarter in appearance, with sparse, colourless eyelashes, and a sharp, enviable nose.

Apart from being somewhat nostrilly, Archie Lively was a likeable, dependable officer but little more. He was a plodder (PC Plodder, his missus called him) good at passing exams, and able to retain enough useless information to impress in most pub quizzes. Last month, he had produced the winning answer to a question so vague that he failed to recall it even now.

"Is there anyone else you can think of who may know of his whereabouts?" PC Walduck asked, fiddling with his smart phone - not needing a little black book. "The neighbours mentioned few visitors."

Andy's landlord had reported his tenant missing over a week ago - sparse mail was backed up against the door - sour, rotted food had dripped through slatted fridge shelves.

There was no record of Andy having left the country, despite the universal text sent to his mobile contacts. His family was none the wiser, and legendary girlfriends were nowhere to be found.

Apparent sexual conquests remained unearthed and - even this last one was tasked with difficulty - close friends were few and far between.

Inspector Lively pocketed his little book as Jean handed him a nice hot cup of tea. A plate of fruit cake slices and Jaffa Cakes was nudged across the kitchen table.

Before accepting the nomination from the Initial

Investigating Officer, Archie Lively had spent most of the week with PC Walduck on traffic detail with the specials. They hadn't mustered a single drunk driver - just a couple of failed rear lights, and an undue care and attentioner. All were duly cautioned - he would probably have let them off if he'd been on his own - too much hassle with the paperwork. Even a seemingly abandoned car on the edge of an estate proved unsatisfactory, its owner discovered nearby with a bat-detector and torch.

"Just had a pipestrelle," the batman had said, "and I was yearning for a noctule."

PC Walduck later suggested heading over to Cannock Chase to check out the dogging but Archie wasn't keen - he just wanted a quiet one.

A quiet one was all he ever wanted.

"We'll check with his various clients and the suppliers," said Police Inspector Lively. "There's no one else you can think of we should contact - you mentioned a Mrs Wisteria?"

"Mrs Lavender — I'm sure Andy mentioned he was doing her garden the next day."

"And this football team?"

"It's a pub team - actually the Horse and Jockey, but I wouldn't say he was particularly close to any of the other players."

"He doesn't like the new centre forward," said Jean. "I remember him saying he was a lazy shit."

That evening, Archie sat at the furthest end of the pub, on a high stool, propped up against the bar, and supped on a pint of cold lager.

He studied the menu, finding little to his liking - the menu barely stretching beyond chips and chicken nuggets.

The barman had been helpful but of little use, not really knowing Andy except as a pub regular - a punter - bit of a knob-head, he said.

A couple of his team mates were equally indifferent to his whereabouts - one suggested he often went missing during matches as well. Alan appeared to be his only genuine friend, but Archie was keen on additional references - details so he could conduct the investigation as efficiently as possible. Just a plodder plodding on.

Andy's account details had dried up before he was reported missing, and the various lap-dancing bars and exclusive clubs that he had boasted about joining proved fruitless with no record existing of him or his credit card details.

All gong and no dinner, thought Archie, taking a long slurp of his pint. This time, his sigh was one of pleasure. There was a burger with cheese and bacon that caught his attention - with something called curly fries. A meeting had been arranged for nine in the morning with the Chief Inspector to review pending cases and performance updates. It was a regular session but one in which Archie was having to become increasingly creative when it came to his input.

Just how much plodding was he prepared to do? He was planning on early retirement in a few years time and if he could remain within the remits of the missing persons unit - with a few light training sessions here and there - then it might be possible to eke out the rest of his service in reasonable comfort.

When Archie got home, there were dents in the armchair cushions where his wife had been sitting. She had been watching the television with her feet characteristically tucked up under her. He slumped down in the chair and pulled his socks off.

Archie wiggled his toes - his feet were a little whiffy but he would have a shower before climbing into bed - he just needed a drink before heading up. He was shattered.

It was good to get back home - and it was getting better with each day closer to his retirement - more time to be had in the shed at the bottom of the garden which, he was determined, would soon be transformed into his own private little den, complete with mini-bar - or at least a cool box - and perhaps a satellite dish.

 He finished his drink, and wearily climbed the stairs to the bathroom. When he did retire, maybe they could get a bungalow.

CHAPTER NINE

It was a drizzly morning, which did nothing to lighten Gill's mood. It hadn't got off to the best of starts with a cat crapping all over the lawn last night. Or was it a fox - don't cats bury theirs?

She resolved to put on some footwear next time. Ripping a hank of paper towels from the roll on the draining board, she wiped gingerly between her toes, curling her lip in disgust. The smell was horrendous. The washing should have been brought in last night but it had been a late one getting back from the Slaughtered Dugong - and she couldn't be arsed.

God, was she feeling grumpy this morning - why did she always drink too much? The rain was getting heavier, fat slugs glistened on the low wall, and the lawn seemed to be getting greener before her eyes. It was a nice little lawn, easily maintained - that's why it severely irked her that some neighbourhood cat had assumed it perfectly OK to take a dump in her garden. Unless it was a fox - they're bastards too.

The damp laundry was clumped in a wicker basket on the

kitchen floor. Her mouth felt half-scraped - she was gasping for a hot drink, and there were only two tea bags left, one with a bit of a damp edge to it. There were some malted milk biscuits around somewhere - she found them by the draining board (where else?) and helped herself to a couple. She couldn't be doing with breakfast this morning - not after all the drinking last night, and made herself a hot mug of tea. Lifting the kettle, she dripped the last scalding drops onto a hapless spider, which wouldn't be climbing up her drainpipe again in a hurry.

She soon found herself thinking about Maddox. It was an odd relationship they had - if indeed it could be called a relationship. It seemed important not to make too big an issue about this lack of ignition - this paucity of emotion and connection.

Gill picked up the empty bottle of wine, and rubbed at a dark ring left behind on the coffee table. Dropping the bottle in the bin, she winced as it crashed to the bottom - it was a stonking headache - a real throbber. Why she had to open a bottle of red last night after three pints of beer she'll never know.

Were these the biscuits that had the two cows on them? Gill couldn't remember. They never really looked like cows either - maybe the one in the foreground did but the shapeless lump in the background looked more like a maggot. In fact, there were two additional shapes - were they meant to be churns or milk bottles?

Sliding a hand across the table, she picked up a book from a pile in front of her. A travel guide to South America with full colour photographs and illustrated maps - she flicked through a few chapters while dunking her biscuits.

Where to start? It seemed ages until the students finished - then she could seriously look forward to a good, long holiday. So many crummy lessons lay ahead, teaching shits like the two James's and the other inbreds.

Alice had been quite sniffy recently when Gill mentioned

going to the Lake District with Maddox. Alice's general indifference made things somewhat uneasy between them, although there had been no simmering stand-off. She was disappointed in Alice, not exactly a worthwhile adversary but it wouldn't do any harm to mark her card anyway - she could actually say Maddox had insisted on them going away together.

She lit another cigarette and coughed vigorously, wiping her mouth with the back of her hand before dunking another malted milk. Who knows, perhaps she could persuade the enigmatic Mr Maddox to come to South America with her.

Finishing her tea in a throaty gulp, Gill filled the kettle and flicked it back on for a re-fill. Deciding on some breakfast after all, she grabbed two thick slices of white bread, and plonked them in the toaster, noticing as she did so that a small smear of cat shit had caught the edge of her hand.

"Bastards!" she said.

Alice decided to call round to Maddox's flat. She had a gift for him, a little something to cheer up his apartment. She liked to think it was a spontaneous visit despite endlessly dithering about it.

"Twigs?" said Maddox.

"Ornamental twigs, I think, but I'm not really sure what you call them. I thought they would look nice in a straw vase by the door."

Not for the first time, Alice found herself wondering what it was about Maddox that tilted this world of hers. What was she doing carting a bunch of twigs around with her? She had met Jackie and Val earlier for coffee and cake at Druckers - they had both expressed some surprise when she piled through the door carrying her purchase.

"Twigs?" asked Jackie, her eyebrows instantly rising to meet the tight, lacquered fringe of her hair.

"I don't even know what they're called," Alice said

helplessly. "I just thought they would look good in a corner somewhere. I thought maybe of giving them to Michael."

"Really?" said Val giddying up a little enthusiasm for, in truth, she was mesmerised by the beauty of the man himself.

"I thought I might drop them round to his flat later - a bit more original than potted plants or knife sets."

"Well, at least he won't have to water them," said Jackie.

"How necessary is it to go bearing gifts?" asked Val.

"She's always been like this," said Jackie. "It was the same at school - always buying little things for the boys she liked."

How the years had flown since she and Jackie had left St Gregory's School, where endless lessons scratched at the tedious day. The conspiratorial huddles and giggles with their best friends Natalie and Molly over a procession of boys, and the shrieking laughter that once followed the discovery of a used condom in the girls toilets.

"I bet its that slag, Bernie - she's been putting out to Karl from the school cricket team," Nat said. "The filthy mare."

"I wouldn't mind a bit of his middle wicket," Molly said.

The laughter - the howling, the screaming and the tears - the never-ending laughter. As it turned out, Jackie married Karl, and Natalie got wed to a bigamist vicar from Rotherham nearly twice her age. She'd heard that Molly had struck more middle wickets than planned with at least five of her seven children sired by different fathers.

Then there was Alice - the thirty-four year old spinster.

It really was time to stop pussyfooting around and get a grip - life was passing her by and the future was shimmering in front of her.

An armful of long, slim, bare twigs seemed the latest thing to furnish a room with - she'd read it in House and Garden magazine (her whole life, it seemed, was metered out in glossy magazines).

The article stated that a bundle of long, thin twigs,

preferably painted yellow with red tips, and tastefully arranged in a straw vase was positively de rigueur these days. A house-warming present to help him settle in the area.

It had been a while since Maddox first started at the college but he didn't strike her as the finicky type - the fact that it had taken this long to make such a gesture was irrelevant, it was a hook on which to hang a hope.

Her other hope - her longed for hope - she conceded, was too young to put bait out for.

"I'm watching you," Gill glowered at a black and white cat padding around in the flower beds. "You so much as fart and this brick is coming your way."

Gill stooped and picked up a wet brick off the patio and weighed it in her hand, daring the cat to squat down. It had stopped raining, and the cat soon wandered off - Gill flicked a little grey slug into the borders.

She couldn't remember the last time she ever went steady with anyone - going steady was something she was ill-equipped to deal with.

To say Maddox was a senior lecturer sort of explained itself - the upright bearing and professionalism, the inviolable authority of the alpha male. But it was a struggle to describe the nature of the man, or the bewildering effect he invoked to someone who hadn't met him before.

"I'm kooky and independent and he can take or leave me," she said, addressing the brick in her hand.

Chuckling to herself, a deep and throaty rasp, she slid back the patio doors and wandered back into the kitchen, and switched the kettle back on - coffee this time, full-leaded - none of that decaffeinated rubbish.

There were still a couple of essays that needed marking before her next creative writing class. She would give them all C minus and be done with it.

CHAPTER TEN

Is there anything worse than a thirsty hen party? Inspector Lively thought there were certainly few scarier sights on Saturday night than these ladies with their banshee shrieks and fluorescent sashes - the L-plates and shredded veils - each party coming complete with an obligatory pub-starved aunt spinning around in their midst.

There was a commotion at the top end of Broad Street, and he hoped it wasn't an offensive weapon scenario - the paper work was horrendous.

Archie recalled a recent stabbing from the previous month when a man had been stuck in the ribs with a knife. He wasn't even on duty. A local butcher who professed an intimacy with blood and the letting of had already tended to the man. Archie had been waiting in the queue at Poundland when the man staggered into the store. The wound had been dressed with a clean bandage from their range of Oudoor Solutions First Aid Kits, which was a total bargain at only a quid. There was blood smeared across the counter, and a trail of gleaming red drips outside.

The man's name was John Smith, which sounded dodgy from the start, and he had been stabbed. This was just about all the information they could get out of him. Outside the store, there was an excited gathering gawping through the window, and Archie was pleased to see the ambulance draw up, followed by a police car.

Archie crouched over the man hoping, not so much to intimidate the man, but to give the impression that he was going about his job - being quietly professional.

"And where do you live, Mr Smith?"

There was no answer, and all the world-weary resignation was born in Archie's repeated question.

"Do you have a fixed address, Mr Smith?"

"Or someone to call?" asked a nearby shop assistant, keen to get into the swing of things.

Fortunately, a friend of Mr Smith was located, and things managed to get a move on from there. He hated the paperwork, which took him best part of the day, but realised the incident could have turned out much worse.

This evening's fracas was suddenly punctuated with someone yelling:

"Leave it Darren - he's not worth it!"

Oh, great, thought Archie, another drunken brawl was in full spate but at least many of the assailants were too sloshed to hurt each other. Girlfriends were screaming from the perimeter. He would skirt around them - they were usually more savage than the blokes.

Someone had pulled Darren off his prey, a black youth who was promising retribution, revenge and, at the very least, a good kicking in the bollocks. Another lad was being laid into by one of the girls, a scary, wire-haired harridan in tight leather trousers and ubiquitous crop top. She had a shoe in one hand, bringing the heel down repeatedly on the back of the boy's head.

What a night - at least he was on a late the next day. If he didn't take the specials out tomorrow, he would head over to Warley Woods with his flask and blanket - have a quick snooze before signing off for the day. He wasn't young - he knew that, and was quite glad not to be. He wasn't keen on too much excitement - the odd weekend punch-up, the odd neighbour dispute, the odd missing person - that would do him.

CHAPTER ELEVEN

The Field Studies Centre was situated on the western shore of Coniston Water, surrounded by tall stands of pine and spruce. Maddox and Gill approached the reception desk but it was unmanned with a sign saying 'Back Soon!'

The best bit of going to the Lake District for the weekend was that somehow Maddox had persuaded the senior management that it would serve as a useful exercise for the English Language and Literature Department. Something about a fact-finding mission to research the merits of writing outdoors, without the constraints of a classroom environment. How he pulled that one off, she'd never know but it wasn't costing her a penny!

Yet another string to the ever-burgeoning bow of Michael Maddox. Had she ever met a man so enigmatic and so emotionally elusive? She was pretty sure she hadn't, but it was definitely worth a stint in the dreary Lake District to get to know him better.

Kayaks, paddles and oars were suspended above the long entrance hall - plastic drums containing an assortment of polystyrene floats, weights, nets, ropes and ballast lay either side of the main doors. Maps with way-marked routes and scored gradients were framed and hung next to vertiginous shots of rope-clad mountaineers on impossible cliff faces.

Although Gill was intrigued, she often feigned indifference whenever the subject of Maddox came up, especially if Alice or the other office girls were in earshot. More than anything, she enjoyed being around him - the reflected association with such a evidently powerful man thrilled her.

Never was sway held so firmly over Tolkien College - such was the studied courtesy Maddox extended to most of the staff, even fat Val thought she might be in with a chance.

However, it did seem the few who didn't adore him (and let's face it - the word is appropriate for he could be charm incarnate), the prevailing emotion seemed to be not one of dislike, or even hate, but one of fear.

Others feared him - they were afraid of Maddox. It would be interesting to see how he got on with the two James's, those troublesome little shits from her creative writing module.

Troublesome - they were little bastards.

"There's not many people about," said Gill.

"I expect they are out and about - doing stuff."

There was a spacious communal lounge with a wood burner, and a couple of garish orange sofas piled high with purple cushions. The huge picture window promised a stunning view over the lake but it was obscured by a tottering mass of conifers in need of a serious lopping.

The main dormitories bled off from the reception area, and Gill wondered about the sleeping arrangements. Berths had been booked for the two of them, and maybe Maddox would think her forward in reserving a room for their sole use but he hadn't given any indication that he expected anything less - or more.

"These bunks are huge - you could easily fit two people into one quite comfortably," said Gill.

"Yes, you could," said Maddox.

The Field Centre had a small bar but they shied away from this, preferring instead the main pub in town, which soon became busy with rosy-cheeked wanderers from campsites and the youth hostel.

Gill was in a great mood, helped along enormously by three pints of best bitter and scampi and chips. Maddox asked about her travels, of which there were many tales, and expressed such an interest that Gill brought along some travel guides the following evening.

The books and maps lay stacked on the table, finger-printed to distraction as a fresh itinerary was explored or route unfolded.

The pub featured many framed photographs of Donald Campbell, and mounted press cuttings of his ill-fated attempt at the water speed record. Maddox was interested to read that after crashing his Bluebird speedboat on the lake, Campbell's headless body wasn't found for another thirty-four years.

There was more - a young woman, murdered by her husband, had been discovered trussed and bound in Coniston Water twenty-one years after going missing. Her body, weighted down with rocks and lead piping had settled on a thin underwater ledge. If it had landed a few metres further from the shore, it would probably have never been recovered. It was a promising lapse in time that Maddox found reassuring.

This lake could do a job for him.

It was very early the next morning, and a silvery sun appeared through the thinning mist as if newly forged from a furnace. A few birds were singing, and a couple of jays called from the wooded shores, their raspy caws strident and harsh. What may have been a thrush delivered clear, fluting notes from the top of a tall tree.

Gill couldn't believe she was out and about so early, and turned to Maddox to say so but instead said:

"What are you doing with that mache..."

These were probably not, if Gill had been able to think about it, the words she imagined as being the last to issue from her lips - the same lips which now lay in a startled 'O' amidst the crumpled features lying in the wet grass where Maddox had shucked off her face with a machete not five seconds hence.

Maddox clutched the cleaver in his right hand, and continued to swish it around as if warming down from a strenuous set of tennis. So clean had been the slice that hardly any blood smeared the blade - just a few drops beaded the sharp cutting edge.

Because he only needed the face - and even that without the ears - he didn't need to concern himself with prising apart any tendons, or teasing essential muscle and tissue from their moorings. A swift upward stroke would take in a good chunk of the chin if she was looking up, so he favoured a downward slice, through the forehead.

As the face flew off her, Gill's legs took a moment to buckle and twist as she twirled to the ground like a broken toy with its elastic cut. Her flaming hair framed an absence of face, which took a moment to pool with blood - thankfully obscuring the mish-mash of hewn bone and tissue.

Maddox was not prone to too much blood before his morning coffee and Twix.

As he picked up Gill's face and brushed off a few stray wisps of grass and some specks of dirt, he was pleased to see a fair bit of attendant flesh still adhered to the back of it. This was good, he decided - it would help keep the shape better. He would freeze it, and excavate the meat as it thawed before shaping it to the skull of his model. He had packed a plastic bag full of ice cubes, and a separate bag for the face.

There was now more blood than he had hoped for so, grabbing a good hank of Gill's ginger hair, he dragged the corpse to the water's edge, letting the head bump along the shingle until it was face down in the shallows. Here he let it bleed out into the water. It would soon clear.

A tiny shoal of minnows shimmered in the water, darting in and out to nervously pluck at any fleshy scraps, the scales on their flanks flashing as they turned in the shallows.

He would have to steer out to the middle of the lake and sink Gill's body later. He wondered about the logistics of this but eventually decided it wasn't worth taking the body back home for grinding.

Thank goodness for Boyd and Hettie Stott and their big grinder. It saved him a fair bit of trouble when it came to disposing of the meat.

Boyd and Hettie owned a smallholding in Worcestershire, not far from the motorway. They were committed to their animals, although Maddox noted a certain incongruity in their practice - a fondness and devotion born in breeding ferrets and rabbits for biomedical research.

He had first come across Hettie Stott at the Sunny Winters Nursing Home when visiting his mother all those years ago. Hettie was a dumpy, sleeve-rolled woman of indiscernible age, and wore apple-rosy cheeks on either side of a small moustache. In charge of the tea trolley, Hettie dished up the hottest brew Maddox had ever known. The first sip had nearly taken off the lining of his throat in a single draught. As he spluttered and choked, Hettie had patted his mouth solicitously with a paper towel and topped up his cup with hot water.

"There, there," he had distinctly heard her say.

He was drawn to Hettie's detached manner, a surreal combination of resigned deference with a blunt, brutish pragmatism. Her body odour - a strong musk of peeled sweat and animal fug - flared up as she moved between trolley and patient. As he wiped himself down, Hettie poured out another cup of tea for his mother who was now sinking deeper in an armchair, bones sticking out of her gown like an old discarded brolly thrown on the kerb side.

With subsequent visits to the Sunny Winters Nursing Home, Maddox deferred to Hettie, and took care with his hot tea and biscuits.

One unseasonably warm day, as he was trying to coax his mother into the garden with a biscuit, Hettie's brother Boyd turned up with a sick ferret. The ferret was a creamy yellow creature with a fading eye mask and glistening wet snout. Rather than wait for Hettie to come home, he had popped the animal into a thick cardboard box, tied it securely to his bike with what looked like an old inner tube, and cycled in to seek his sister's advice. Maddox was struck, not just by the fact that someone had wheeled in a sick ferret in a box, but that Hettie's brother looked exactly like Hettie but without the moustache.

"He's got a bit of a runny nose," explained Boyd to his sister who had been busy doling out cups of tea to a line of residents on the patio. "And he bitted me!"

Maddox watched on as Hettie wound a short gauze dressing around her brother's bleeding thumb. His hands were stumpy and gnarled, grimed with dirt. They stood together, with matching grey socks and scuffed shoes - short and squat and holding a scraggly old ferret between them. Hettie returned to her tea urn, and irritably dashed out a few more cups.

"As if I haven't got enough to do."

It turned out that her brother also worked at Sunny Winters occasionally, helping out at weekends in the extensive grounds. It would have been too grand to describe him as a gardener or even an odd-job man, but he could often be seen hoeing around the old Victorian rose garden that lay beneath the buckled windows of the old house.

Thinking back, Maddox was sure he had seen him on his first visit to the nursing home - the time he brought his mother - skulking behind an old garden shed. He had thought Boyd one of the patients - rat-like, rodenty, but perhaps more ferrety now he came to think about it.

At the time, his mother had been pulling on his sleeve, rubbing her face, and asking who he was - where was he taking her?

The Sunny Winters Nursing Home had dominated the view from the long gravelled path, a tree-lined route where Maddox and his mother stood hand in hand before walking up to the main doors. Reams of low flattened bricks of beige and cream were stacked from one end of the rise to the other, with a fall of terraces descending to the driveway. In the centre of the complex was a small tower, stumpy and apologetic, with a clock clacking and whirring but definitely not chiming.

A bit like the patients, Maddox thought. She had clutched his hand tightly, pulling against him, not wanting to continue. Her elbows held rigid and square, with her short steps stuttering and tentative like the hands on the clock. His mother had eventually allowed herself to be led into the care of the doctors and nursing staff of the home, and it would have been a sad day indeed if he had felt sad about it. But the remorse would come later to puzzle and confuse him.

Instead, it had been with an overriding sense of equanimity that Maddox delivered his mother into the asylum.

It had come to such in the end. It was no surprise and yet Maddox still remembered feeling a little bewildered afterwards, as if he had lost something, and then suddenly remembered he had given it away in the first place.

It was at the newsagents - or rather outside the newsagents in the city centre, when Maddox finally realised that his mother needed help. That his mother had started putting the furniture of her mind out onto the pavement.

"Stay!" he had said.

"Stay!" he had said as if talking to an unleashed dog.

And she stayed. Like an unleashed dog. Trembling and moving gently from one foot to the other as she waited for him to return. He looked up from the queue, and watched her moving around in a world of her own. Where had she gone, his mother? - his beautiful mother with her pale eyes, with her soft-smelling skin and creamy complexion. Her white, so very white and silky-soft hair.

But all he could see was a husk with even whiter, frosted hair, hot-lidded eyes and thin lips - skinny legs barely hanging on to their exhausted tights. Her face a mask, an utter blank.

Not long after, he received a telephone call at three in the morning from police who had found his mother walking around the streets in her nightgown looking for her long-dead husband.

By the time Maddox reached the house, a young officer had tucked her up in bed with a cup of cocoa. Maddox remembered being impressed that the young officer had gone out of his way to do this.

Using the grinder on Andy had provided several meals for Boyd and Hettie's ferret colony, dutifully mixed as he had been with bone meal and rusk. However, it hardly seemed worth the trouble to lug Gill's body back to the smallholding - especially as there would be some local harvesting to be undertaken anyway.

In the end, Maddox decided to pitch Gill's body out into the middle of the lake using one of the kayaks from the outdoor centre. He had taken the largest kayak out earlier the previous day, a bright red vessel with painted shark's teeth on the prow, and moored it further along the lake shore.

A slight breeze ruffled the mist, and the lake was pricked with a million shards of diamond light. Gill's head, clotted with gore, bobbed and slurped in the lapping wavelets.

Under cover of the mist which, even Maddox with his meticulous planning had to admit was very convenient, he set off to retrieve the kayak, the grinning shark's teeth gleaming white among the rushes.

He bundled the corpse aboard and paddled out into the cold empty expanse of Coniston Water. The mist still blanketed the lake, and the shark-toothed kayak was low in the water. The vessel keeled sharply as he hauled Gill's body overboard, freighted with weights tied to both feet. It was a pity about the hair. It was so luxurious, a real thick mop of ginger but it wasn't what he was looking for. He had in mind a shade darker and richer - a fulsome, thick setting for his project. The face required cushioning in a luxuriant surround, like a piece of jewellery in its own little box. A dark brunette would do, or even black - preferably pitch and glossy, and shimmering with little electric jolts of blue which always seemed to shoot through such hair.

Yes, black - thick, black and lush, but definitely not ginger. The fish could have that.

There was a very satisfying plop as Gill spiralled down into the depths, her blood-matted hair sucked down with her like seaweed down a plug hole.

At least he didn't have the face staring back at him as she went - that was carefully stowed away in his rucksack.

CHAPTER TWELVE

Alice swept the thick, black hair from her eyes, and collected a sheaf of copies from the printer. She wasn't walking quite so elegantly this morning on account of the new shoes she had treated herself to at the weekend. Following advice from the fashion editor at Cosmopolitan, she had opted for slightly elevated heels with purple stitching along the welt but they were really pinching into her now - and one of the straps had also come undone. Such as it was with Alice and shoes - they never really got on.

"Funny that - Gill taking off to South America without so much as a bye-your-leave," said Jackie.

"Mr Maddox said she just upped and left after their weekend in the Lake District. Couldn't even be bothered working her notice," said Val, leaning back in her chair and reaching for a box of Jaffa Cakes. "I doubt if the college would have her back now - even if things didn't work out for her."

"Mind you, it does leave the way clear for someone to have

a pop at Mr Maddox," said Sandra, who was sporting a new array of love bites this morning.

"They weren't really going out," said Alice. "They were just good friends."

"Any more clichés we don't know about?"

"These are hardly fattening at all," said Val, holding up a Jaffa Cake.

"Mr Maddox is covering the creative writing classes until they get someone in from the agency."

"I reckon he knocked her back, and she couldn't hack it - that's why she's gone off to Brazil."

"Bolivia - Mr Maddox said she was planning to go to Bolivia."

Val got up and walked to the far end of the room, her rolling eyes suggesting Alice should follow her. Out of the window, a few students could be seen milling about. Val gave a deep sigh - it was getting dark, and she could feel a bit of Seasonal Affectation Disorder coming on.

"I hate this time of year," she said.

"I like it," said Alice. "Season of mists and mellow fruitfulness and all that."

"Mellow mists were weeks ago - now it's cold and dark and dank," Val touched her throat with a podgy finger before putting to rights a cactus on the window sill. "I feel I can talk to you, Alice, I mean really talk - I feel we've known each other for years."

"We have, Val," said Alice.

"Then you must tell me, and tell me honestly - do you have any designs on Mr Maddox?"

Unrequited love is so exhausting, thought Alice, and soon she found herself thinking once more about David - always David. Was there room for anything else lately in that befuddled mind of hers? Every time she thought of him she would crush the image, tamping it back down into her subconsciousness. At the weekend, she had bumped into him in the precinct, and such was the jolt that shot through her body, the blood sang in her veins. She didn't welcome the sensation, all fuzzy and whirly - her chest tightening as if coiled with steel hawsers.

Frantic shoppers sped by, child-laden buggies bullied their way through the crowds, and Alice clumsily leaned in so close that he actually took a step backward. His beautiful, beaming smile negated any awkwardness as she ooped, and said something about having rubbish balance in these heels.

"They're new," she said, holding up a plastic carrier bag with her old shoes in. "I thought I might walk back in them - break them in."

"Nice shoes," said David. "I like the purple thing going on."

All the feelings rattling out of her were genuine - not the premeditated gush of a girly crush, or the calculated starburst of glossy magazine-driven angst.

The conviction spurred her on - she knew she wanted him but hoped it was the unattainable aspect that appealed - the inaccessibility of desire - surely this was the irresistible force behind her obsession?

She desperately wanted to taste those lips - they would hold a hint of freshly crushed spring grass, or maybe cinnamon from some recently quaffed Cappuccino. She would slurp off the froth from those lips and sieve it between her teeth and, by God, she would give him the tonguing of his life.

"No, no, Val - no designs whatsoever," said Alice.

Hawthorn James Smethwick never knew what possessed his parents to name him after a tree.

He wasn't best pleased, either when they insisted he repeat the module in creative writing at Tolkien College - especially as the module leader - that bitch, Preston - seemed to hold a personal grudge against him.

Fortunately one of Hawthorn's middle names was James and, in a subconscious homage to his best friend, he answered only to this name, and they subsequently became the infamous two James's.

In their first semester at the college, a student had teased Hawthorn James about his unusual first name, and was immediately battered with a hole-punch (some hysterical students claimed they had actually seen brain matter). Afterwards, there was the small matter of a suspension, and a letter of apology to smooth things over before he could return to the college. There was also an undisclosed donation to the Tolkien Alumni Fund made by his father.

Hawthorn James's tantrums could never withstand the molten threat from parents who vowed to deny him computer games, WiFi and various satellite television subscriptions unless he complied with their wishes. Wishes? More like demands, he pouted.

His parents were learned academics - doctors in pharmacology who both travelled extensively, heading off to various conferences to present cognitive-behavioural papers. He would be left home alone for days, with food, plenty of money, and contact numbers in case of an emergency. The arrangement suited him - not being taken with parents in general, and his own in particular.

He sat at the back of the classroom, and launched a fierce glower in the direction of Maddox who had only just informed the students that, for the time being, he would be covering the creative writing module.

Ms Preston had apparently gone off to South America to find herself.

"She couldn't exactly get lost," said Hawthorn to his bestest-ever mate James Jones. "Not with all that minging ginger on her."

James Jones sniggered and slowly expanded his snigger into a full-throated impersonation of Gill Preston's rattling laugh. It was quite good actually.

Maddox raised an eyebrow.

Ah - the two James's, he thought.

"Ah - the two James's." He said.

The two James's beamed. Neither of the boys would end up doing justice to their photographs when they were later published in the national press after having been missing for months.

The more she thought about kissing David, the more Alice convinced herself of its eventual possibility. Lads drink alcohol, that's what they do. She and David would get drunk together, and one thing would lead to another - they could always laugh it off later as a mad drunken episode. David would be gracious, as he always was, and she would have a wonderful memory in the bank to draw on whenever she wanted to.

Alice thought about it for a moment - no, she certainly wasn't above such a thing if that was what it took. She'd seen him tipsy a few times, his lovely ringing laughter rising in little eddies as he slugged at a can, or levered a slice of pizza from the box.

If David took the initiative, that would be even better - and Alice wondered, not for the first time, what it would be like to sleep with him. She imagined him on top of her, his frothy Cappuccino breath coming in short abbreviated bursts as he swept his lips across hers, her hands straying down his lean back before scooping over his tight little buttocks. Would he have that little baize of hair nestling in the small of his back like so many of her lovers? (So many? - scoffed Inner Voice - what planet are you on?) She had caught sight of his midriff one special summer afternoon, and it was surprisingly hairy, a jostling of bristles licking up to the naval.

She would lie him on his back, mantling him like a bird of prey, and brush him with electric swatches of black hair. A flickering, scented candle would pick out her glossy blue highlights. She imagined narrowing her eyes - she was the predator here - and jutting out a jaw to catch his lower lip in a firm but gentle grip, looping her tongue into his willing mouth.

He never wore shorts in the summer unlike Simon who was always baring his legs even in winter. Were his legs muscular and tanned? Alice wondered - there was so much to explore - so much lying in wait for her.

Maybe they were little bleached sticks of celery with no muscle tone to them, or calf-heavy - perhaps even mapped in eczema? Alice found herself almost wishing he had something wrong with him, a defect - bad breath or dandruff - or wheezy with asthma. Anything to make him less appealing for even his faults would garner interest - blemishes that needed smoothing over. Sour breath in the morning suggested a night spent together, and nothing could taint that prospect. Maybe he had a couple of unsightly moles clutching at his flank, some skin tags braiding his upper arms - a cyst punched into his back. It would be of little consequence to Alice who, much to her dismay, would welcome bereavement so she could fold him in her arms - offer comfort. How ill it behove her, she thought, to entreat tragedy for such ends.

She stretched at her desk, like a cat awakening from a particularly mice-laden dream. Deliciously shaking off her fantasy, she reached for her mobile phone.

A flyer for an arty event at the Sunflower Lounge lay on her desk, and she was going to text the details to David.

It would read: Fancy it? Alice. X

Mr Maddox was, Hawthorn conceded, annoyingly adept, and at the end of the lesson both lads had felt completely outflanked - cheated out of petty disruption. Maddox had effortlessly deflected any antagonism thrown at him, and even had them joining in a discussion on the art of good style.

That couldn't be good.

When James Jones proffered that Ms Preston was nothing

more than a bag of old ginger shite, Mr Maddox extended the metaphor over the course of the lesson, and invited contributions from the class so long as they contained a variant of 'old shite' and was wary of clichés.

"Clichés," he said, "are the enemies of good style."

The two James's hunkered down at the back of the class, trundling out as much mumbled derision as they could muster.

James Jones was not blessed with anything approaching good looks, owning a particularly enormous mouth, which caused his eyes to close whenever he swallowed anything. A resident wad of chewing gum shuttled contemptuously from side to side.

The other James was short and hated being so. He had a beguiling smile that crinkled his eyes - a disarming feature that masked an intent that could not, in any way, be referred to as wholesome.

"This is just a waste of time," said one of the James's.

"Complete load of bollocks!" said the other.

"Indeed," said Maddox.

Hawthorn slouched down in his seat, cargo trousers rucked up around a slim torso. It was the torso that Maddox latched upon but dismissed almost instantly as being unprofitable. However, he didn't necessarily need the skin - what lay beneath could be harvested, if required.

There was an awkwardness about the class at first, but Maddox sliced through the discomfort with an airy assurance. It was as if an unspoken stand-off had been declared - two great beasts circling around a water hole - but whereas the two James's postured and preened, Maddox positively burned with the prospect of locking horns - his lean face suffused with a simmering darkness.

Insolently, Hawthorn grabbed his own crotch and had a bit of a jostle, hoping to embarrass Maddox but he merely suggested that if he wanted to masturbate, to go right on ahead and have a good tug.

Hawthorn's cheeks reddened as the class laughed - and a class schooled in creative writing can laugh in very creative ways.

"I could have had him up for sexual assault," Hawthorn said afterwards to his mate who seemed strangely preoccupied, if not a little subdued.

"He was sort of OK really, when you come to think about it," said James Jones.

"No he wasn't - he was a fucking cu..."

"The way he managed to get the class reacting like that," Jones cut his friend off with a hand held up to be talked to. "It was almost interesting - I would never have thought adjectives could have such a deadening effect on descriptions."

"Well I think he's a right dirty old bastard, more or less asking to see my todger and all."

"He was just messing that's all - better any day than that mouldy old bitch, Preston - God, I hate her!"

It was true enough - Gill Preston had a nice line in sarcastic one-liners, and an implacable contempt for the students. She also had handouts, often sitting on the edge of a table, doling out reams of information sheets and printouts. It was all she could do to stop herself yawning. Any handouts that came the way of the two James's were summarily scrunched up and cast behind the radiators. If they caught fire, that would be a bonus. The college could burn down for all they cared.

"It was almost as if he could reach into my soul," said James Jones, eloquently outlining his most creative output for several years. "It was well weird."

"You've lost me mate," said Hawthorn hitching up his waistband a notch. "I think he was a right tosser!"

"Like I said, better than that bitch."

The Sunflower Lounge was buzzing, crammed with what could best be described as an eclectic mix. The speakers were pounding, scattered groups of shabby youths were huddled over low tables and imitation-leather cubes. Others were gathered outside in little smoking cliques, and Alice was relieved to see a few older individuals shambling around with drinks held aloft.

She was grateful to be crushed up against David, away from the door and in one of the darker recesses of the bar. A fug of cigarette smoke kept wafting in from outside, and the volume of the music was so high that each time David turned to speak to Alice, delicious flecks of spittle flew against her cheek.

His eyes, those glorious syrupy eyes with attendant lashes, were slowly glazing. It was probably as much to do with the rogue cigarette smoke as the alcohol but Alice was hopeful that it wouldn't be long before a closer level of intimacy was reached.

She had never, ever felt this way about someone before.

Well, maybe twice before.

There had been Joel, with his soft northern accent that enchanted her so much at university. He had been a considerate, gentle lover (now he did have that little scrape of hair in the small of his back - how she used to pull and tug at it). Before Joel, there was Gary, with his gappy smile and bitten fingernails.

But neither of them made her feel like the way she did with David. He was slowly succumbing to the evening's lull, gently swaying into her as she took his hand - a hand so cool and responsive that Alice couldn't resist giving it a gentle squeeze.

When he responded with a slightly stronger squeeze of his own, Alice's knees nearly buckled, and it was all she could do to stop herself yelping.

Was she willing to risk their budding friendship with a kiss? Alice sipped on her gin and tonic. Someone had told her that the tonic gave you bad breath in the morning. Would that be an issue?

David was smiling as he took another swig of lager, his full lips glossy and ripe in the blue smoky light of the bar. Alice leaned into him, charging her face with what she hoped was an impression of suppressed bliss and contentment. It was quite a feat. There was the faintest acrid smell off him that she hoovered up and it made her shiver.

The kiss - Alice so wanted the kiss. To consume him, the fullness of him - who ever said never wish for what you want, it may come true? There was nothing she wanted more than to taste those lips. She leaned into him, her mouth slightly parted, a breath against a windowpane.

David turned to her.

CHAPTER THIRTEEN

David's kisses bore little trace of cinnamon. They were crushing and violent, slobbery and wet - almost careless in their urgency. With his beautifully lashed eyes closed tight against hot lids, he gently grazed the taut, quivering skin with his full, wide lips. His breath was sweet, coming in stuttering exhalations, and the quivering impetus of his lithe body brought forth muffled gasps beneath him.

Almost at once followed tender kisses, the slightest brush of a lower lip evoked a demented euphoria. Soft whispery breath soughed between them as fingers were slowly suckled, or soft fluted skin nuzzled. Occasionally he would pause for a moment before drawing his mouth, lips misshapen by the flesh beneath him, along an arm to worry aimlessly at the hot skin beneath with his pink tongue. His eyes remained closed, beads of sweat popped up at his forehead, perspiration filmed his chest and shoulders and, from the gentle hollow of his lower back, drops of moisture dewed the fine downy fluff that swept up and over the ridge of his firm buttocks.

"How was it for you?" he said, looking down and grinning.
"Wonderful," said Simon.

James Jones had been well and truly bemused by Maddox's mesmeric performance but it had little to do with style and grammar.

It was the dark look in Maddox's face that had shuddered the very foundations of James Jones' being. A look so dark and evil, and brimming with such malevolence as to send delicious ripples of electricity snapping up his spine. The manner in which the lupine smile unwound without even stirring the Stygian depths of those eyes had James concocting a mental shrine at which he felt compelled to worship.

Could nobody else see it?

His best friend - the other James, if you will - was mischievous and insolent, a tad childish but pleasantly mean-spirited. Then there was this curious lecturer on another level altogether. That shuddering look of Mr Maddox was truly evil incarnate. It was what James Jones had been waiting for - it was what he had been waiting for, for a long time.

James Jones had graduated through all the fledgling rites of passage - school, the tedious first crush, sticky under-the-mattress magazines, inseparable best mates (all of whom changed and separated with each passing week, it seemed). A brutal arrogance and disposable vindictiveness forestalled any budding alliances. Playmates and peers dwindled by the wayside, often with the accrual of several bruises and Chinese burns.

Hawthorn James had been the only friend to last longer than a year, sharing as they did an almost infinite appetite for mayhem and mischief. But mischief was too trite, too cosy for James Jones now - too primary school. It wasn't that he craved more - he simply needed more.

Bane of the creative writing module they may have been,

but the two James's were gaffed by Maddox, and thrown gaping and floundering on the deck, hooked and filleted by the bewildering charisma of the man.

For James Jones, there were few enduring experiences that defied the passing of time, but there was nothing in his back catalogue that gripped him so tightly or so surely as the indifferent cruelty of childhood.

Of course, there had always been the never-ending thrills of pulling the legs off Daddy-Long-Legs - amputations that surely should be accompanied by a satisfying twang - and watching the limbs twitch and jerk on the hot yard slabs. Such joy was there in prising wing cases off ladybirds, and letting the thumbed bodies spin to the ground. Drowning wasps in sticky tin cans was always a favourite - angry yellow and black furies bristling their rage as they mired in sweet dollops of strawberry jam.

Such rejoicing was also to be had in the yellow mulch pus of squished slugs slammed between house bricks.

In the hot afternoons of the long summer holidays, he would set about collecting spiders, ants and beetles in jam jars. Carrying his collection into the garden shed, jars would be emptied into a glass tank, and he would writhe with gladiatorial glee if the creatures fell upon each other. All too often though, the insects and spiders would scuttle over each other with indifferent haste and he would have to pour boiling water over them in a rage of disappointment.

Fat earthworms were a favourite of his - with these he couldn't lose. He pulled the glistening gloops of worms from the wet earth, rolled out the fattest ones on the floor of the shed, and stuck them with thorns twisted from his mother's prize rosebushes.

It was a natural progression from bugs to amphibians. Soda straws pushed into frogs, toads skewered, newts dangled over flames until the squirming stopped, and the crackling and smoking began.

And then there was the kitten.

It was a little black and white thing, hardly weaned and always mewling. Five minutes on full power had done the job.

Back home in the tidy suburban semi with its tidy suburban garden smothered in shrubbery and wisteria, James Jones would look out beyond the white fence towards the garden shed with wistful nostalgia as he remembered those good times, recalling the desolate rapture afterwards when he looked down on charred remains and gristled debris.

He needed these little distractions. Just like the other James, he was an only child of eminently professional parents, both dental surgeons who were forever leaving him alone to attend their London practices. They would return home with jars of spiced almonds, bottled piccalilli and torn theatre stubs.

Sometimes - and it was never in the dead of night, always in the glare of the long day - his imagination bloomed, and he would fantasise about really hurting someone - seriously hurting someone.

He realised that the other James had been displaced by something more potent, more vital and alive - a thing brimming with venom. Even his lurid imagination couldn't quite capture the black look of those eyes as he tried to conjure the darkling depths beneath that brow, and a frisson of undiluted ecstasy scampered under his skin as he realised that the one person in the whole world who could give his barren, empty life some purpose was Mr Maddox.

Mr Maddox, he was convinced, would know all about the hurting.

Where had Simon come from? Was it the muted lighting in the Sunflower Lounge that plunged her into a reckless sense of self?

Did she really want to dupe herself so senselessly at her age? It was pathetic. (Don't start! She warned Inner Voice). Afterwards, she tried convincing herself that it was the mix of alcohol, dim lighting, and the chalky fug of the place that downed her defences. Defences she had had no intention of putting up in the first place.

Matching David drink for drink had unhinged her in equal measure but no matter how guarded she refused to be, there was residual satisfaction in the outcome. There had been little doubt about it - he was definitely about to respond to her overtures.

Then Simon had turned up. Where had he come from - had David sent him a text?

David had responded and that was the main thing. The way he had leaned in - it was the only thing that mattered - he almost planted that luscious mouth on hers. Would it have been a wet, red snog like some wide-lipped sea creature grazing on coral, or would there have been diminutive, tender snips? Maybe he would have cupped her face in his hands and snogged the face off of her. Forever filed away in her own personal bank was a new dimension to an emotional account that cried out for further exploration - how would he have kissed her?

Simon seemed a little sheepish when blundering across them, as if he couldn't believe what he thought he almost saw. Alice detected in her brother a little pinched moue of disapproval.

Why would he be so disappointed in me? Thought Alice.

"Mate!" David's glassy eyes took a moment to register before he reached out and gathered Simon into a chummy embrace that instantly excluded her.

"Me and your sis were having a moment," he slurred - big, wide lips munching the words.

"You're so pissed!"

"...and you're so ugly but in the morning you will be sober."

Within minutes it was as if nothing had happened. Simon and David were draped over each other - and nothing had happened.

Alice thought she should have let the taxi take her all the way home after leaving the Sunflower Lounge but opted instead to get out and walk the last stretch past the cemetery. She left David and Simon to the excruciatingly loud music of the bar, which continued to boom. Her eyes were rimmed red and, after checking her reflection in the mirror, decided it wasn't a look that suited her.

It was late, her head felt fuzzy but there was still that same sense of mild euphoria burrowing into her.

How pleased she had been to see some recent pimpling around David's brow, some latent acne that had suddenly popped up since the last time. It was a mark of imperfection, which Alice relished - a sign that he wasn't too perfect for her.

Simon seemed so drab compared to David but her brother always had good skin - just bad teeth. She was very fond of Simon but a violent stab of hatred had pierced her when he turned up.

In the cemetery, several new graves lay fat in the moonlight, waiting for the earth to settle before stones could be put up.

Beyond the crumbling brick walls grew a yew tree, and the shadowy bulk of the church lay behind its taut foliage. In the tree there was probably an owl. The church gates were buckled and ancient - she could never remember the gates ever swinging open or hanging freely - always they seemed twisted into the very earth of the cemetery.

Alice walked slowly, breathing in the cold damp air, and enjoying the mothy night, relishing the solitude and the dreams it bore.

She took a short cut through the tomb-stoned enclave, nothing daunting her now, buoyed as she was with prospective thoughts of love and promising futures.

What if it just didn't work out? Was she destined to tread such a soulless path through life, pining for what had never been hers in the first place?

She was definitely too old for all this pitiful lamenting.
Perhaps Michael Maddox would be the better option after all. If David didn't work out, she thought, there would always be Maddox.

CHAPTER FOURTEEN

In the cool of his apartment, Maddox sat across from the dormer window, enjoying a large malt whiskey. He grinned repeatedly at the new chest freezer that lay - proud, white, blocky and gleaming - in front of him.

Freezers of this type required more floor area than the upright ones but are more economical - or so the salesman had told him. These freezers lose less cold air each time they're opened whereas in upright freezers, the cold air flows down and out.

The salesman had been on song. To eliminate any unpleasant odours, the inside of the freezer needs to be washed with one tablespoon of baking soda in two pints of water, or with one cup of vinegar in a gallon of water.

Maddox had bought plenty of baking soda.

He put down his whiskey, and opened the freezer. Fish fingers were flanked by broccoli and sweetcorn - tubs of ice cream lay on top of lemon sorbets, and several bags of ice cubes were frozen together in frosty clumps. All were slightly glazed with ice, and as he lifted out a bag of mixed veg, flakes of frost fell gently onto Gill's face.

Maddox was reasonably satisfied - it was an altogether more pleasing face than that of Andy. In the end, he had decided against throwing Andy's face away - it was scrolled up and stored alongside some herrings at the bottom of the freezer.

Stretched out underneath the baskets of frozen food lay the life-size model skeleton from the science department, loosely clothed in various people.

Maddox was still not convinced about the fitting of Gill's face, which was pulled tight across the skull and held with two thick elastic bands. The skin wasn't stretched enough - it still retained a certain elasticity, and had started to flare at the edges whenever he defrosted it. He had swapped it several times with Andy's face over the last few days, even pulling the skeleton out and holding it up to the light to discern favourable textures. He would tip it carefully, and mull over lighting and angles for his project - the soft curves that held the shade, the gentle dips and hollows that pooled with shadow.

The thing with Andy's face was the substantial scorching it had incurred when Maddox tried to iron it onto the love doll. Why he hadn't thought about using the college skeleton in the first place was still a source of mild irritation to him. After all, has there ever been a more perfect vehicle on which to drape skin and park organs than the human skeleton?

It was important not to recreate with exactness - there was scant satisfaction in producing a work so perfectly unblemished and lifelike that it might as well have been real. It was all in the interpretation - and the quest, of course - the indefatigable searching and yearning of the true artist.

Maddox's particular quest for good thighs had caused him more than a moment's reflection on the folly of discarding Andy's legs so readily. They were easily the most agreeable seen so far but he had thought them a little on the chunky side at first. Eventually they had been ground down for

115

Boyd and Hettie's hungry ferrets - the femurs, in particular, being something of a trial to dispose of.

The more he thought about Boyd and Hettie, the more pleased he was that he'd cultivated their friendship during the many visits to the Sunny Winters Nursing Home. Not once did they ever question his deliveries, or even look into the bags - on no single occasion did they insist on operating the grinder themselves. It wasn't that they lacked curiosity - it was just something that didn't interest them greatly. There was always fresh meat for the ferrets, kindly supplied by Mr Maddox who claimed it was surplus from his uncle's butchery business - and that was all that mattered.

Once, when he visited his mother during the last year of her illness - those long drawn-out months before she went into hospital - Hettie was washing his mother's hair, and they were both laughing as she worked up a lather. As Hettie towelled her dry, she mussed up his mother's hair, and told her that her lovely son Michael, was waiting to see her, and he'd brought some nice magazines with pictures in. He had looked at the magazines - they may as well have been for children - comics for all the good they'd do. On the cover of one, there was a picture of a young woman sitting on a kitchen stool, smiling at her own mother in the background. Maddox later looked into the ward. His mother bristled in the pillows, sucked into the mattress, sticks of bones pinioned to sleeves.

The magazines were scrolled up and dropped into a bin.

Maddox emerged from his lingering reverie to lift a few more items out of the chest freezer, before squaring the bags of mixed veg with sweetcorn, and lining the small tubs of ice cream into a more agreeable arrangement. Satisfied, he paced over to the thin mantelpiece surrounding the black-grate fire. Propped up on the corner was a small, framed photograph of his mother. White-haired and shining with happiness, she smiled into the camera, a bloom of late afternoon sun sealing the moment.

Maddox's mother had been wearing a pale blue nightgown with tiny cornflowers sewn along the hem. The shock of white hair teased up into a candy floss coiffure without any trace of dye or colour was a fluffy little bonnet of cotton against the blue walls of the ward.

Slumped in a chair beside the bed, thin bones spiking up the pale blue gown, her memories scuttled and floated aimlessly in a blue world. Occasionally, little fragments of the past would rise, spluttering to the surface and then, just as suddenly, sink back down into the depths.

"You know I love you, Mikey."

"I know Mom."

"You were my favourite son."

"I was your only son."

"You are just like your father - he never liked squirrels."

"How are you, Mom?"

She had her good days and her bad days but the good ones became fewer and further between. Sadder by far were the more lucid hours when his mother would fix him with eager beady eyes as he walked through the ward and sat down next to her bed.

"Mikey, I don't like it here."

He would hold her gnarled little hand in his bony paw and stroke it, as if to transfer his own vitality through blue, tissue-thin skin. Her arms were crackly and skinny - little winter sticks of kindling; there was an ocherous stain under her chin, which the nurse's flannel had missed after lunch - probably soup, or a sweet mash.

"Take me back home, Mikey, please."

"You're best here, Mom, just for a little bit. I'll come and take you home when you're better."

"But I don't like it here, Mikey."

He set some fruit on the bedside table, and slipped a new nightgown into the drawer.

"I'll ask the nurse to change you into this tomorrow, if you like? It's blue - your favourite colour."

"I like pink."

Before long, he began to favour the brevity of his mother's awareness, it being easier to leave when she was looking out of the window, laughing at squirrels.

"Goodbye, Mom."

Eventually, he stopped looking back after leaving. His mother would rarely look at him either, nor watch him as he left the ward. Her sweet little face, soft rubbery parchment scrunched into gleeful self-absorption, constantly watching the window.

Maddox turned back to the freezer and removed another couple of baskets so he could better appraise the project in its entirety. There was no hair assigned for the head yet but black would definitely be his preferred choice - this, he was sure, would accentuate either of Andy or Gill's pale features. Ginger was a definite no-go despite the ruddy tresses suiting Gill so well - and strawberry blond was obviously out too. There was no neck or shoulders or chest yet, and he reckoned some nice sprung ribs would be an ideal setting to store various viscera. Some of the internal organs could be visible in the final rendering for he was considering the possible use of a panel - a hank of dried skin or desiccated tissue to create a small textured partition, which could be opened or closed if desired. It was a radical departure from the original concept but nevertheless consistent with the ongoing evolution of the project.

It was a shame about those delicate hands of Jonathan Mortimer's, but he did have some very satisfactory feet courtesy of an early morning walker.

For some time now, the large shoes of a man that he sometimes encountered when enjoying a morning stroll along the Harborne Walkway had intrigued Maddox.

On more than one occasion, Maddox found himself casting sly glances at these shoes whenever he passed him on the walk, marvelling at the massive low-heeled brogues as the man scuffled his way along the path. Those shoes could well be harbouring feet of some distinction, and the man often marked Maddox with a cursory nod and smile as they passed each other on the thin lane.

The Harborne Walkway was once an old single-track railway line in the fifties and burrowed a green, leafy way through the suburbs. Regenerated into a cool wooded corridor on the outskirts of the city, it was much favoured by joggers and dog walkers.

It was the latter that concerned Maddox most after he had turned swiftly, and stove in the man's head with a brick. The last thing he needed was some mutt nosing around in the undergrowth before he had a chance to recover the body.

He gazed down at the feet, at those impossibly large brogues canting askew on the lifeless legs of the stricken man. Fortunately it was easy to roll the body down the embankment, and hoist it over a fence where it clumped down in the small bird reserve running parallel to the walkway.

The brick was matted with dark hair and gore, unsurprisingly sticky after the bludgeoning. Rolling a few strands of the clotted hair between his long, bony fingers, he dismissed it as being neither lustrous nor black enough. Collection of the body via some adjacent allotments was a mere formality - a wheelbarrow and some old, threadbare fertilizer sacks provided all the cover he needed to shuttle the dead man round to his car.

Maddox had only been after some supplementary tissue - a few bits and bobs to shore up some gaps in the upper body, and soon he had the body back at his flat, spread-eagled on the plastic dust-sheets and ready for exploration.

Untying the laces, he pulled off the shoes that he had admired so much, and was gratified to discover that his instincts had been correct for the feet were staggeringly beautiful - toenails immaculately pedicured and buffed, with

119

the little toes not turned in but padded with bulbous fleshy nodes. The ankles were to die for - packed shields of skin capping tight knuckles of bone with the tendons taut like ship's hawsers.

Maddox pulled down the trousers in hopeful expectation that maybe the feet were a natural continuation of equally perfect thighs and shanks. Perhaps he would only need to joint the body from the waist down. He ran his hands along the legs. They were very white, popped with little blue veins on the inside, and quite thin up to the rather knobbly knees. Also, he thought, they were a little too much on the fleshy side for the thighs, which made for a unusual combination.

With the indifferent dedication of a surgeon, he tugged the man's underpants down. The man's penis was something to write home about. It lay at length alongside his right thigh, tubular and uncut, and untroubled by the weight of the sagging scrotum. This was a little disconcerting for Maddox. He was ambivalent about the gender of his finished piece or, indeed, whether the piece required any defining sexuality. It certainly wasn't worth considering at such a rudimentary stage but would he later regret not harvesting it?

In the end, he decided against lopping off the member, and instead turned the body over to appraise the buttocks.

These were far from pleasing. Although not particularly hairy, which Maddox deemed essential to the whole dorsal ensemble, they were a little on the podgy side. He needed footballers' buttocks - or those of a similar ilk - a muscular and toned sports pair - a natural by-product of an athletic persuasion from which he was also confident of gleaning the thighs he needed.

He pulled the corpse into a sitting position to examine the lower back. There was little to glean from this area and he released the body - there was no need for further exploration. The head jounced with a hollow thud against the floor, starring the sheets with smudged rosettes of blood, the arms slapping the carpet as if sockets had no say in the matter.

The feet and shins were all he needed - the rest could be jointed and crammed in the freezer for Boyd and Hettie's increasingly busy grinder.

CHAPTER FIFTEEN

"Kitty!" his mother laughed as a couple of squirrels chased each other up into the trees.

The signs had all been there. Maddox recalled the never-to-be-forgotten time when he caught her looking quizzically at her hat.

"What is it?" her brow crazy-paved in puzzlement.

"A hat, Mother, your hat."

"I must be going senile."

She had laughed then.

Another time. Not long after the hat:

"What do I do with this?"

"It's a pen. You write with it."

She laughed at that as well but there was no joy in the sound.

She started to collect pencils and pens, brightly coloured sticks - and kept them in a shoe box by her bed where each morning and evening, she would empty the box, and line them up along the lipsticks and creams on her dressing table. Lipsticks, she learned, were also good for the writing, and she hoarded these too. She would line them up with the pencils in order of length from the longest to the shortest. Then she wouldn't line them up in order.

Then she began to eat them.

Maddox found himself confiscating her pens and lipsticks and the eyeliners - for she found she could write just as well with these too.

"Let me take these," he would say gently but her fists would suddenly bristle with pens as she clung on tightly to her possessions. He would have to distract her, promise her a favourite television programme or a biscuit - suggest looking for something she may have lost - where was her blue cardigan? Her fury was explosive but easily doused, and Maddox became adept at defusing her anguished mind.

Maddox would lead his confused mother to her bedroom but she wouldn't let go of him until he promised to bring the shoe box back into the room. His mother didn't seem bothered that there were no pens or pencils inside the shoe box. She couldn't remember ever having pens and pencils in the first place but the shoe box remained a comfort.

Who is this woman? Maddox thought, looking at his mother as she curled her way into the sheets. This cored remnant of someone who used to be loving, kind and blessed with a gentle unhurried manner.

He remembered eating pears with her in the garden, of looking deep into cereal packets - scrabbling for the plastic toy. Is this really the woman who took such joy in his childish paintings - his crayon drawings and potato prints - his crude dinosaurs and orange, spiky suns? This mother who told him that he would be a world famous artist - the mother who whitened his gym pumps, and sewed badges on his school blazer. The one who never failed to ensure he had the Beano every Wednesday.

He had hired carers to look after his mother at home but she didn't trust them. They would cook and clean for her but she was convinced they were trying to poison her.

Then there was the incontinence, and the wet, sodden

armchairs. The doctors believed a number of small strokes may have led to her dementia - they recommended Sunny Winters Nursing Home with a revolutionary programme of mental stimulation that she could undergo.

His mother had been an intelligent and independent woman, and odd snatches of her past would occasionally bully their way through this dense fog of confusion. One afternoon, her bedside radio was playing an old song, and she sang every lyric perfectly. Sometimes, he would pick up a magazine from her bed, and the crossword would be completed. She would smile and giggle, and point out of the window at the clouds, or the squirrels as they chased each other in the top branches.

He had been asked to report to the main reception at three o'clock, before the patients had settled down to their tea-time. He could stay with her if he wished - it would only be something light, something with warm milk and medication.

Maddox had in his other hand, a brand new suitcase with her spare clothes, and the empty shoe box. There were blue cotton pyjamas, and nightdresses too.

There were other brick outbuildings scattered around the main building as though added on as afterthoughts. Neat squares of lawn were contained within the high enclosing walls, a few with wooden benches underneath spindly trees; a copper beech shone at the top of the terrace.

A ratty-looking man - the gardener or a patient - peered out from a wooden shack, and suddenly withdrew back into the shadows and cobwebs.

At the main door of the building, he rang the bell. A spy hole blinked, and he imagined a single eye inspecting them before numerous locks slid open and half the door was opened. In the entrance hall, the porter sat himself back behind a desk, and drew out a ledger. The porter had been reading a newspaper, his hands inky as he smudged a finger down the ledger.

"I'll be back on Wednesday," said Maddox.

He hoped she would be proud of him - proud of his dedication and resolve - the energy invested in this undertaking of his - the task that he had set himself.

CHAPTER SIXTEEN

"So you play football?"

"Yes - and tennis and squash."

"You must be very fit."

"I must say I do like to work out - I run half marathons too," said the interviewee to Jonathan Mortimer.

Mortimer and Principal Richardson had both conducted the initial interviews for the vacant lecturer's position not long after it became apparent Gill wasn't returning from Bolivia any day soon. They had been a sorry bunch, and Richardson was happy to let Mortimer choose his own appointee from the short list of two.

So it was either the sporty Stephen Snodgrass ("I spell my name with a ph") or the crop-haired Liz Something-or-other, a boss-eyed essayist draped in flannel zebra jammies, a burnt orange trench coat, and wearing floral-patterned boots.

Unless Stephen Snodgrass with the ph managed to spectacularly self-combust, the job would be his. Of course, he would need to ask Maddox his opinion before he confirmed the appointment - it would go without saying.

"There's every possibility," said Mortimer, stretching out his small hands so the light gleamed off his buffed cuticles, "of a team-building exercise in the Lake District - this would be undertaken in the Easter or summer holidays. There's no obligation to attend but..."

"I climb and abseil as well."

"I thought you might."

They were in Mortimer's office, and Snodgrass unfurled his long thin legs, stretching them out in front of him. There was an animal ease in the manner with which he conducted himself - almost cat-like, unlike the wolf that was Maddox. Mortimer wondered what it would be like to be compared in flattering terms with a wild animal.

Mortimer had discussed the team-building exercise with Maddox at his house not so long ago. The programme had shown rather a few too many office types chasing through mud, scuttling under low nets and tottering across rickety logs.

Having sanctioned Maddox and Gill's earlier jaunt to the Lake District, Principal Richardson suggested that Mortimer might like to organise the team-building session for staff development purposes.

"Hopefully we won't lose any more members of staff," he said sourly before moving off.

The principal's recent interest in the Great Outdoors was due to the governor of a rival college - the Tony Hancock Institute of Enduring Studies - being given a recent slot on local radio and television where she had waxed lyrical about a team-building initiative in Snowdonia. This was apparently already paying dividends in high morale and stunning academic achievement - absenteeism had also been reduced to an all-time low.

"There's no details yet but I expect it will be somewhere in the Lake District - or the Peaks but not in Snowdonia."

Mortimer was captivated by Stephen Snodgrass's astonishing Adam's apple, which bobbed up and down as if

127

conducting some independent abseiling of its own. Considering his athletic prowess, Snodgrass was rather thin - especially those legs - gaunt and whippet-ribbed. His hair was greying with a lighter streak occasionally sweeping down across his face - a face rich in cheekbones and sharp brows.

Mortimer could easily see him scrabbling up rocks and crags, clawing at trees. He looked down and contemplated his own unfair paunch - unfair because he hardly ever drank, and ate reasonably healthy.

Maddox had a flat stomach too. Like a greyhound - or a wolf or a fox or a jackal - there was always something canine about him - something unerringly lupine. Even that sharp eyetooth of his could worry an elk bone.

After Binky had bitten him, Maddox had been solicitous and considerate, yet strangely detached from the whole incident, as if from another dimension altogether. Just before the dog had taken a bite out of his hand, Mortimer had experienced a vague feeling of unease, a sixth sense almost, as if something terrible was about to happen - and it had.

Mortimer was bored now, and this man Snodgrass was tedious beyond belief. Not at all engaging like Maddox had been. Still they needed a replacement for Gill, and he didn't want some cross-eyed psychedelic nutter galloping around the department in big, flowery boots.

"The job is yours," he said.

Boyd and Hettie Stott were in the main holding room when Maddox turned up with a fresh consignment of meat. The meat was cut and jointed and wrapped in several layers of newspaper, bundled in bin-liners and stashed in the boot of his car.

Hettie rolled up her sleeves before scrubbing the food pots, rinsing them under the tap, and clattering them upside down on the draining board. The sweat dripped off her, and she was looking forward to a nice bath - one of these days. It was part of the reason they had to let her go at the Sunny Winters Nursing Home. It was unfortunate that, when surrounded with the piss, the swabbed benches, and rich carbolic smells that stained the very walls of Sunny Winters, complaints of an unhygienic nature should ever have been levelled at her.

The Board of Governors' attention had been drawn to a couple of complaints about her being a bit on the 'whiffy side' from visitors and colleagues. There had even been a wry smile and a few chuckles when the Acting Chairman pointed out that she was a 'bit ripe' but when the Princess Royal, after opening the new extension to the East Wing, had been heard to complain that there was a smell around here like a 'dead horse with a decomposing corgi shoved up it's arse' that drastic steps had to be taken.

"More nosh for the boys," said Maddox.

He moved past them into the vast utility room, plastic bags sagging and sloshing as he carried them through. The room was a large open area with a bare concrete floor. On a long beaten bench running the length of the far wall were a couple of electric food mixers, a small autoclave, and the grinder.

"I'll grind the meat up myself - save you the bother."

"I'll make us a cup of tea," said Hettie.

CHAPTER SEVENTEEN

Inspector Lively was familiar with the Tolkien College of Continuing Studies - he recalled mediating a local conflict or something involving a couple of their unruly students - the two Johnnie's, he seemed to think.

After everything had been settled, the principal invited him to take a place on the guest speaker rostrum, and extol the attractions of a career in the police force. He used to finish with 'May the Force be with You' until a colleague at the station said it was a pretty lame way to end a presentation, and everyone seemed to agree with him.

He was now standing in Principal Richardson's office, with PC Walduck, trying to discern the whereabouts of a missing teacher.

"She was last seen in the Lake District with Mr Maddox, one of our English lecturers."

"Is Mr Maddox here at the college?"

"Yes, I'll have someone fetch him."

Richardson asked his secretary to find Mr Maddox, while Inspector Lively unsheathed his little black book; PC Walduck shook out his smart phone. Archie was getting the hang of this missing persons business, which was infinitely preferable to marshalling drink-sodden hen parties between bars and clubs.

The door to the classroom had a small window through which Maddox could watch the new lecturer settle down to his lesson. Large windows on the opposite side flooded the room with sunlight.

Stephen Snodgrass nervously opened his briefcase, fumbled through a few papers, and took out a batch of pastel-coloured paperbacks.

Examining each slender volume in turn, he chose a slim blue one with the author's name embossed in silver.

A familiar lupine smile edged the corners of Maddox's mouth. There was a slight catch to Snodgrass's voice as his thin, lipless mouth grew tight.

Maddox was keen to check out any potential contributions for his project - this work of his that was so much a work in progress. He needed some thighs and a wholesome pair of buttocks, but there was little to glean through the window, except to surmise that such acquisitions would not be forthcoming from this particular person.

Snodgrass's face suddenly twitched, and his mouth pulled into a little purse of disapproval.

Maddox assumed - quite rightly as it turned out - that the infamous two James's were somehow at the root of that disapproving moue. If only he could snare such a dramatic device - the sheer engineering apparatus of facial expression - all those internal wires and pulleys that sucked the mouth into a little puckered pit. But such animation did not lend itself to the enterprise - there would be no tickling of neurons and receptors, no massaging of electrical impulses.

Snodgrass was getting flustered. Maddox could see the colour rising in him, the pinkness flushing up from his throat where the alarming Adam's apple thrashed about like a fish in a keep net. He longed to harness such a reaction

131

for his project, it would elevate the whole ensemble to a new level but it was folly to think such machinations could be successfully incorporated within the final framework.

He considered the finality of his work and it did not rest easy with him. The creation required continuous appraisal, a series of evolutionary links that should, in essence, have no end result but rather be augmented, reupholstered and renovated over time. Maddox sighed - perhaps it really was a work of life and not his life's work.

"Mr Maddox."

It was Principal Richardson's secretary, calling to him from across the corridor.

The two James's were very pleased with their morning's work - the slow dismantling of a new member of staff had gone very well. They had pretty much excelled themselves with the melted Mars bar - it would take more than a dash of washing powder and bluey whiteness to get those stains out.

The new lecturer had gone very red, and the crimson hues of humiliation and despair were colours so very dear to their hearts.

The class had finished but there was no hurry to get to the next one despite the late attendance rule, which stipulated students couldn't enter a class if they were ten minutes late. No one ever implemented the rule and whoop-de-do if they did.

The delicious afterglow of a job well done, the two James's high-fived each other, and made their way out into the corridor.

Hawthorn James was a little disquieted after rising from his customary slouch to celebrate with Jones. Although loathe to admit it, he was secretly appalled at having to stretch to reach Jones' offered hand - not quite but almost on tip-toes. He watched as his best friend walked ahead of him through the doorway, aware of how little he had grown himself these past couple of years. There was little doubt that Jones had stolen more than a march on him in the height department. In their first year at the college, there had been little difference between them, although James Jones was always much the stockier of the two. Fatter, some would say.

It was only recently that he had noticed this - there had been two students in the desks in front of him, and he could swear they had grown a foot each in the last year - and one of them was a girl! The previous week, a tall girl with beaded dreadlocks had pushed past him, and called him a crib midget.

Fucking bitch, he had said, before the girl slammed him in the bollocks with her tote bag and pinned him to the wall with a knee.

Hawthorn James was becoming impatient with the stunted growth thing, he was as lean as a cat but his mate was bulking out, as were the other students. Soon they would no longer be the two James's but the fat one and his scrawny little sidekick. His best friend seemed so preoccupied these days too, as if he was up to something - but they were always up to something together, weren't they?

Hawthorn's father (when he was there and not gadding about at some psychopharmacology conference) said he'd end up flipping burgers or delivering flyers unless he got a grip - pointing out that he was at college, not school - no longer a schoolboy but an adult. Well, if he hadn't inherited his father's stumpy genes, and grew a bit taller, he could maybe take this adult theme seriously. As it was, he looked more like a school kid than ever.

Looking around, he saw that Jones was no longer to be seen - his best friend had gone and left him behind. He looked both ways along the corridor as if about to cross a busy road but there was no sign of Jones anywhere. Well, he would just have to be late on his own then.

The police officers were two men.

It was not long before Maddox wondered at the possibility of utilising the incredible nostrils sported by the older officer - dark circular holes with the collars of each nostril stretched as if bound with wire - they twitched momentarily.

"Mr Maddox?" the older, nostrilly officer greeted him. "I'm Police Inspector Lively, and this is PC Walduck."

"Good morning," said Maddox.

"Just a few enquiries - nothing to worry about."

"I never worry."

Principal Richardson indicated that they should sit down but they remained standing.

"Ms Gill Preston," began Inspector Lively, his practised demeanor somewhat rattled by Maddox's ice-cold composure. "I don't suppose you know where she is?"

As opening gambits go, this wasn't Archie's finest hour, but those searing green eyes and snaggle-toothed smile had already begun their work.

"Do I know where she is - or where she said she was going?"

"Either, I suppose," said Inspector Lively.

"Bolivia, I believe - at least, that's where she said she was going."

"And she didn't return with you from this..." Inspector Lively snapped his little black book open and shuffled through the pages.

"Fact-finding mission in the Lake District," offered PC Walduck, his smart phone blistering with efficiency.

"Yes, the Lake District," Inspector Lively snapped his book shut. If nostrils could bridle, they were saddled up with resentment.

"We were exploring the dual possibilities of incorporating a field trip into the language and literature modules, as well as sourcing a suitable location for a team-building opportunity, and no she didn't."

"Didn't?"

"Didn't return with me."

"Did she say she was definitely intending to leave the country?"

"There was no doubt about it."

PC Walduck spun through some Apps on his smart phone looking for something to impress.

"We were in a pub at Coniston - the Black Bull I think it was called. Ms Preston brought along some maps and books about South America. She seemed very excited about leaving but I didn't realise she intended to leave quite so soon."

"And that's all you can tell us?"

"Is there any more to tell?" asked Maddox. "I was as surprised as anyone when she failed to turn up for breakfast the next day."

"But weren't you sharing a room?"

"Yes, it was one of those hostel type rooms - she must have left early before I woke up. I got up quite early myself to go birdwatching, and she wasn't in her bed. I'm afraid I can't recall whether the bed had been slept in."

"He likes his birdwatching, don't you, Mr Maddox?"

"I do, Principal Richardson - I'm quite partial to a bit of twitching."

Inspector Lively and the other one thanked them for their time, and walked back to their car.

"Do you think he was telling the truth?" asked PC Walduck, keen to jemmy a reaction from the set of his superior's face. It seemed to PC Walduck that Inspector Lively was readying his flawed yet formidable resources to repute Maddox's testimony.

"Oh, I expect so," said Archie.

Inspector Lively did not want to lock horns with anybody - least of all someone like Maddox - when early retirement was looming. He told PC Walduck to contact the landlord of the Black Bull, see if any additional information was forthcoming. He fancied an early pint in the Swaddled Duckling - his latest favourite pub, and arranged to meet PC Walduck there later.

At odds with most people's perception of him, Archie couldn't stand real ale - not for him the stinky enclaves of cask-conditioned retreats with their farty atmospheres and woollen pullovers. He enjoyed nice fresh bars with expensive fizzy draughts of indistinguishable lagers.

The Swaddled Duckling boasted a range of continental lagers and, when PC Walduck finally joined him, they worked their way down the bar until they reached the San Miguel. He couldn't stay much longer though - his wife had a corned beef hash on the go.

"I love corned beef hash - especially when you mash in all the gravy and give it a good stir."

They downed the last of their drinks and made ready to leave.

"He was a bit of a strange fish, that Maddox," said PC Walduck.

"He was a bit odd," conceded Archie, "but he doesn't strike me as anything sinister. If you ask me, this Preston woman just upped and left - did a runner."

"But her credit and debit cards haven't been touched for ages. Something must have happened to her."

"Well, all we can do is make enquiries - sometimes, some people just don't want to be found."

Subsequent enquiries at Tolkien College failed to unearth anything new other than Gill Preston was a popular - occasionally exasperating - colleague. There was some suggestion that she and Maddox may have been linked romantically but the associations were tenuous at best. It was almost as if the staff refused to believe such a liaison was credible.

Alice was hopeless at sublimating.

Once again, having thought she had got over David, there

was that old familiar blow - that snappy little low punch - when she wandered into the lounge.

He was with Simon, watching television. They could have been reading books or magazines, or eating pizza - it really wouldn't have mattered. She envied their cosy, companionable world.

Alice sat down at the table, and casually asked David about his course, and how he was getting on - a contrived nonchalance that didn't fool her heart, which hammered away.

Increased heart rate, breathing rate, metabolism, muscle tension - all increase with attraction, she thought, having read about the symptoms in a particularly acerbic issue of Cosmopolitan.

David was wearing a striped grey cardigan over a white tee shirt with those low-slung jeans hanging off his arse.

Damn it! She had been considering a possible move into the eminently more suitable Michael Maddox territory, but was forever getting snared by David. Maddox really was quite a catch when she thought about it (and her mother made sure she did). Alice wondered just how necessary it was to have an all-singing, all-dancing, stardust-sprinkling sensation with someone. How much further could she elevate her relationship with Maddox above the simple trusting friendship that it was so far - would it ever reach the heights that she yearned for with David?

Alice would meet Maddox at his apartment, where they would open a bottle of wine. Occasionally, they would venture out to the pub, or to the cinema if there was something good on. Their conversation didn't need to stir any depths - rarely would she feel anything other than a pleasant evening had passed. He had even given Alice the spare keys to his apartment so she could let herself in.

"It'll save you hanging around if I'm stuck in another meeting," he told her, and Alice clutched the keys, enjoying the cold, hard feel of them. It was a shame Gill was finding herself in Bolivia. If ever there were keys to be jangled around the office, these were the ones.

It had been some time since Alice last received a text from David, and it was a relief that she relied on such a fillip less and less.

Hopefully she was moving on from her hopeless infatuation - her relationship with David, she had decided, was now going to be one of gentle introspection and regard.

That little inconvenient thing known as a 'reality check' was constantly popping by and shaking her out of these ridiculous reveries. It was inconceivable that David would ever feel the same way about her - it was impossible. Without that constant in her life, the vacuity and aimlessness of a single existence was rinsed and hung out to dry. The appeal of being so independently single that always had been so shuddering in its conviction, now felt a little tenuous, like the last gossamer strands holding a web to its moorings.

Nevertheless, she still found herself walking to the college canteen and thinking about David, and not Maddox - would he be sitting down to lunch, or making do with the vending machine? It was as if whatever he was doing would shape her own choice. If she imagined him eating a cheese cob with pickled beetroot, she would choose the cheese cob and pickled beetroot - if he opted for the Cappuccino with sprinkles, then so too must she.

Alice knew such a similar scenario would never be sought with Maddox, no matter how fond she became of him. That was the difference between fantasy and reality. It wasn't just a case of keeping her dignity - she had never lost it, but she relied on a heckling realism.

Was life really too short to wait for returned affection?

As she rounded the corridor from the main foyer, Alice saw the new lecturer fiercely scrutinising the notice boards. He looked rather flustered and red.

Alice walked over to him.

At the end of the lesson, Snodgrass had grabbed his books and his papers and stuffed them deep into the briefcase before snapping it shut - there was still a fair bit of sniggering going on as he left the classroom. He was the first one to leave the room.

"Sir, you've shit yourself, sir!"

Those words will remain forever scorched in his mind.

As he stalked down the corridor, his long strides pumped with adrenaline - his mind seared with indignation. He found himself blushing as he recalled the humiliation - the gurgling mirth of students who shook and howled - yes, howled with laughter (and he swore he could see them shaking!) How had he not noticed it in the first place? He had stood up and walked towards the whiteboard, feeling a slight tug on the back of his trouser leg. There, sliding down the back of his trousers, was something that looked like a severely chewed bar of chocolate, which also looked like - and there was no getting away from it - a shit.

It clumped to the floor.

It was a melted Mars bar. He must have sat on it - probably unwrapped and placed there while he was busy sorting out the books and handouts for the lesson.

After that there was no chance of getting them interested in the first chapter of Flaubert's Parrot.

"It's not about a parrot," he had blustered. "It's an exercise in postmodernism."

But they were more interested in the Mars bar.

"Sir, you've done a skiddie!"

After leaving the classroom, he went straight to the staff washrooms to sluice the ugly, brown smear from his trousers. He held his leg up to the dryer and frantically pawed at it until the stain lifted a little. His face burned as he paused at the end of the corridor and pressed his forehead against the cool wall, the lick of rogue grey hair sticking up like a bobtail. Realising that his departure might have seemed a little too hasty, he considered returning to the classroom and making light of the incident but it was too late now. The staff and students who passed were too preoccupied to notice him but occasionally, almost out of earshot, he would hear a whispered enquiry as to who he was. He studied the notice board intently as if searching for a particular item.

A pair of bleached Goths and a few hoodies shambled past him. One of the girls from the main office - Alice or Alison, he seemed to think her name was - had seen him and was walking over. He realised he was standing in front of the Gay and Lesbian Society noticeboard, and quickly shuffled over to a board dedicated to sports and activity clubs. Pinned to it were images of laughing students as they plunged through white water rapids in colourful kayaks, or launched themselves from viaducts on knotted ropes. A lurid, lime-green poster promoted an upcoming orienteering competition, with little dockets of contact numbers pinned alongside it.

"You're the new English lecturer aren't you?" asked Alice.

"Yes." Said Snodgrass.

"I thought I recognised you - are you lost?"

With his Adam's apple scuttling up and down his throat, he complained about two particularly obnoxious students in his class today, one of them fat-mouthed and wide-eyed, the other much shorter.

He didn't mention the molten chocolate bar incident - it was all too embarrassing.

Alice could see the way his thin mouth became agitated, like a thin fishing line snapped across a rushing stream. Lowering her face, she looked up at him with her baby blue eyes which were, in reality, shit-brown.

She said it must be quite an ordeal taking over from Gill Preston who had run away to find herself.

"Nothing I couldn't handle," he lied, having been very close to a nervous breakdown.

140

In the staff room, with coffee and a shortbread finger, Alice talked with Snodgrass some more, thinking him as ordinary a man as you could hope to find with such a thin mouth, flat voice and dull eyes.

Maddox, whose own eyes betrayed little in the way of emotion, could flood them with energy whenever he spoke. Phrases could flutter, light and airy as vespers, but when his eyes were little more than pinpricks, his voice slid and scraped across open spaces.

Alice glanced across the staff room, distracted by the very voice she had just been thinking about. It was Maddox in close conversation with Jonathan Mortimer - another who had succumbed to the ferocity of his charm. Mortimer was wearing his usual pristine clean, white shirt starched within an inch of its life, and seemed to have had his hair cut in a new style, short at the sides and layered on top.

"I'm liking the hair," said Alice when they made their way over to the small kitchen area.

"Really? I tried that new place in the precinct - I fear it may be a little too trendy for me."

"Not at all," said Alice. "It suits you."

It looked a bit like Maddox's hair in the way it was styled but it wasn't as thick, and didn't fall so naturally about the nape.

"We were just discussing the team-building trip to the Lake District," said Mortimer.

"We are considering a short trip up there soon - just to check it out, put in place the various events - team games, archery, paint-balling, abseiling, crossing a river using oil drums - that sort of thing," said Maddox.

"Any rock climbing?" asked Snodgrass.

"Well, that's what we need to find out. Mr Maddox has recommended a lodge quite close to Coniston where he and Gill stayed - before she buggered off to Brazil."

"Bolivia."

Maddox was wearing a two-button jacket over a pale

yellow Lacoste shirt, a pair of easy linen trousers and his faithful leather slip-on shoes. Not quite the beating heart that needed stilling whenever she was around David, but there was a spiky feel good sensation the more she looked at Maddox these days. So maybe it was possible to make herself fall in love with him - there was no disputing she could do a lot worse.

"Who will look after your dogs?" Maddox asked.

"They'll be fine - it'll only be for a few days. I'll ask Mrs Fenshaw next door to keep an eye on them - she absolutely adores dogs."

CHAPTER EIGHTEEN

Alice and her boyfriends:

When she was six, there was Tony, a little black lad with Bambi eyelashes, and hair like charred crinkle-cut chips. After her tenth birthday, she was smitten with Douglas, a pale copper-haired lad who suffered with eczema, and frightened her with tales of having little cuff-sewn cotton gloves when he was a baby so that he wouldn't scratch himself to death.

At the ripe old age of thirteen Alice had shared her first kiss with a boy named Nigel Percival, a name that suited him perfectly - prim, oiled black hair and a shiny plump face, which shone like wax and even had little spots of red on each cheek.

The kiss had seemed a very adult thing to do at the time, and she remembered feeling very grown up afterwards even though it was the merest bumping of lips, like those kissing fish she had once seen in the aquarium at the zoo.

Her first real kiss, a full-on snog with Mark Webster from the lower sixth had her gasping for air and reaching for the Polo mints.

Throughout school there was always one boy or another bringing little gifts, for she had been an attractive girl before the dowdiness set in. A packet of fruit pastilles one week, a bar of chocolate the next or, when she moved up to secondary school, individually compiled audio tapes with music meticulously pulled from the radio, or even the latest chart-topping single. When the gifts dried up, she would ply her own for favoured boys, issuing tokens and treats with over-arching nonchalance.

At university there were the two great loves of her life - Gary and Joel. Before these two, no one lasted more than a few months - maybe two terms at the most. Joel hooked her with his soft northern vowels and ferocious blushing. Joel also helped Alice to get over Gary.

Gary had never meant to be cruel, it just happened - him and Lisa falling in love they way they did. The last thing he wanted was to hurt her but he had fallen for another - they shared a bond, him and Lisa - they had met, he said, when reaching for the last croissant at a cafe. They couldn't help themselves - it wasn't her - it was him. Fill in the blanks...

Gary played squash and loved rock music, which was something of a surprise for his whole demeanour was one of the cello or piano. When Alice, in a moment of swooning indulgence, showed her mother a photograph of Gary with his gap-toothed smile closed to an angelic, inscrutable twinkle, she commented on how sweet he looked - almost cherubic.

Gary wore brown corduroy trousers and they often joked about him being at the cutting edge of fashion - he never minded her gentle chiding, although she really did wish he would wear something else - something a little bolder.

I see you're going for the history teacher look this morning, she would sometimes say, before enthusing about block purples and savage yellows.

He was found dead one morning, not long after they had graduated - something to do with his heart. Only twenty-three years old. A young couple had found him - face down in the park. Alice's grief had known no bounds. There had been floods of tears, despite the fact that he had dumped her for tarty Lisa with the horn rim spectacles and the big nose.

Joel was a different kettle of fish - always fumbling and frowning, with a scratchy little voice and a smile as wide as his face. He hated his nose and was always commenting on it because it was slightly crooked. They were always laughing, her and Joel, but after a while, the register of their mirth became jaded and worn, faded laughter giving way to tight smiles, and before either of them knew it, they had outgrown each other.

Then the dowdiness began to set in.

It was painful, this love business, and it took a while before Alice eventually decided she could well do without it.

Following one particularly brutal weekend of needless yearning and introspection, she sought out Val for a bit of a chat.

"I need to re-evaluate what's important to me in life."

"What do you mean?" asked Val, not unreasonably, who was already in the process of evaluating a selection of Hob-Nobs and chocolate fingers on a plate in front of her.

"I just don't want to go through life wishing I had never taken a chance."

"Taken a chance on what?"

"I don't know - life? Love? The chance to be happy or not to be."

"Happiness is not a pre-ordained condition, Alice, sometimes things happen."

"How will I ever know if happiness awaits me if I'm not prepared to take a chance?"

"Hmm, sounds like you're building yourself up to ask someone out."

It irked Alice that someone so seemingly unconnected with the policies and politics of the office romances - which virtually happened by rota these days - could be so unerringly spot-on with their observations. She watched as Val hoisted herself out of the black swivel chair and taxied down the office between the banks of desks and computers to the coffee machine. She felt slightly bewildered and frustrated - Val was someone she could confide in, or express doubts to because her frame of life experience seemed so limited as to afford Alice a sense of profound worldliness in comparison. That was why it was so irritating that Val had been so accurate in her summations.

She watched Val pour herself a coffee, add milk from a carton, take a huge gulp and top up the mug again. She hovered over the sugar bowl, a couple of colleagues on either side hesitated behind her like vultures at a lion kill, patiently waiting their turn. Val soon returned, interested to know whom Alice had in mind, fervently hoping it wasn't Michael Maddox.

"No, it's not Michael. It's no one specific," she lied.

Val pulled out a plastic sandwich box from her bag and prised off the lid - it was time for her mid-morning snack. Inside were cubes of Feta cheese on a bed of lettuce, some radishes, a rolled-up slice of Pastrami with a few scoops of cottage cheese spooned over it, and a couple of green things - possibly gherkins or olives. Also from her bag, Val plucked a couple of cellophane-wrapped pastries bursting with layers of white cream and almonds.

"If there was such a thing as a perfect man for me, it would be Michael Maddox," said Val.

Which got Alice thinking if Maddox was the right man for her after all. Even if he was, it didn't necessarily follow that she was the right woman for him.

Maddox held court with Principal Richardson, discussing ornithology and habitats. He also orchestrated lesson plans with effortless ease, presided over departmental meetings, and discussed mayonnaise-based sandwich fillings with Bridget and Connie from the college canteen.

It was all so easy for him.

There was also another aspect to Maddox that she had grown more and more attuned to over the past few months - he was quite fit. Maddox never mentioned playing sport or going to the gym but there was an athletic leanness to him, a loose-limbed bearing that carried him aloft - almost predatory in its demeanour. Clothes fitted him as if clipped to a sartorial blueprint, and beneath those cuffed Gabardine trousers it was easy to imagine tight sinewy hams and buns of steel - you could almost sense the interlocking joinery of polished muscle.

Maddox was immeasurably pleased with his thighs and buttocks. He admired them for many minutes - the tautness of them, the tight sheaths of muscle that slid underneath the skin like gloved spearheads. Smooth hairless lines curled along the length of peerless thighs.

He admired them so much that he picked them up and carried them over to the window for a better look, setting them down on a small picnic trestle table he had picked up in town for £9.99.

The twin trails of blood from the tourniqueted stumps were quite negligible, and would be easily wiped clean with a cloth. Above the waist where he had lopped off the hips with a bow saw, the staunched mulch of bloody gore was padded with cotton and gauze after being bled out over the sink.

It had been a much easier task than he thought it would be, but by cutting straight down through the lumbar vertebrae, it was relatively simple to prise away the flesh by parting the natural seams of muscle and tissue with a sharp blade.

Sometimes, Maddox thought to himself, that when you stopped looking hard enough, the answer would just pop up of its own accord. For a while now, he had consigned himself to scouting around the parks and playing fields for some suitable buttocks. Thighs, he decided, would be a

147

bonus but he was also reasonably confident that both thighs and buttocks would come as a single package.

There had been no football games being played on the evening in question but there were some lacrosse games in progress, and a little hockey on the peripheral pitches. Hockey, he realised, could be worth watching with many of the players having to crouch low to strike the ball - a great one for building up the muscle tone in the upper legs. A few of the players looked suitable - he could have been spoiled for choice but they did seem a little top heavy in the thigh department.

Maddox favoured the cellulite-free offerings of the male leg although he knew there was potential in the orange peel-free zones of a young woman. He was about to leave when a blonde six foot, three inch girl on the adjoining lacrosse game dramatically drew attention to herself by calling an opponent a fucking spaghead!

She was stunning, a Valkyrie, with long tanned legs that poured from a thin waist, hardly a knobble at the knee, and a pleasing tapering to the shins as they tucked themselves into brilliant bright white socks. A short white-pleated skirt rode over the light heft of her bottom with only the merest nubs of a pelvis causing the skirt to fan out whenever she strode forward. White knickers too, noted Maddox with vague disinterest - possibly the only item, he recalled Andy telling him, which could enhance the natural beauty of womanly flesh.

It was a shame then that he had to cut off her feet - they were really rather poor with scrunched up toes and slightly fungal nails, but at least he now had something to attach his recently-harvested feet to.

Since he first spied her, Maddox had taken to watching her for several weeks, initially from the road but later observing her discreetly from the bushes and hedges that grew along the perimeter fences. Peering through binoculars, Maddox scanned the wide field of pitches. The binoculars were small enough to hold in a handkerchief - always at the ready to nonchalantly sneeze into should he come across any voyeurs in the rhododendrons.

She was always the last one to leave the changing rooms (no doubt, those legs needing a good lathering), and she was supremely confident as only a six foot, three inch Amazon could be.

The few games he had tailed her, the team never lost, and on only one occasion had they come close to losing. She was without doubt the team's biggest asset with aggressive posturing, and arrogant leadership but her aloofness also meant that, regardless of her sporting prowess, there were seldom any friends waiting around for her after the match.

To her credit, Carolyn didn't seem in the least bit bothered by her teammates indifference - winning was all that mattered to her, and she didn't give a shit what the others thought.

Maddox knew her name was Carolyn because he asked her just before swinging the Lacrosse Warrior shaft into her face, snapping back her head and driving several teeth up into her gums. He was impressed with the shaft's flexibility, it had the combined strength and feel of carbon composite, and he enjoyed the heft of the material as he took it back over his shoulder and drove it back into her soggy face. She fell to her knees and wavered slightly, a look of glazed astonishment fading from her already-clouding eyes - her resilience was impressive. It then took little more than a few final clubs with the stick to crumple her to the ground.

Blood spread out, matting the grass in thick black-red blood as he pulled her into the bushes and wrapped some of the attendant foliage around her. No one would have seen a thing - they had been suitably screened from the road by a mass of mussed vegetation, and the far edge of the deserted pavilion was shrouded by a hard line of laurel hedging.

It was settled. Alice would have a cut-off point - it would be Wednesday.

She would tilt once more at David, and if there was no response, no flustering reaction - not even a flicker, then it would be time to move on. She was at that blurred, gauzy stage where she definitely didn't want anything to cling to - wanting to be completely through with the straw clutching.

Alice was lying on her bed, with her coat still on after a quick circuit around the park to blow away the cobwebs.

Staring at the ceiling, she breathed deeply, holding it in and breathing out slowly. She stayed like this for a few minutes then got up, took off her coat and looked around the room as if discovering it for the first time.

Although she had her own place - a small, two bedroom flat in Bournville - she would often choose to stay over at her parents. There was a sadness to her childhood room and she cultivated it, wanting the happy sadness of nostalgia to seep into her.

The bed still had the Miró print cover on it from her university days - bright blues and orange scribbles; there was a bedside cabinet, a thin rug, a small chest of drawers with a framed mirror propped up on it, and a portable television bracketed to a corner of the wall. The walls were originally painted magnolia but were now an oily cream colour with patches and squares of light where furniture had been jostled around and rearranged. Outside the window, the tops of lime trees swayed in a light breeze. At bedtime, as a child, moonlight would throw their shadows across the bedroom, and she would make out shapes of animals on the walls and ceiling before drifting off to sleep. She switched on the lamp and a bark of light snapped across the surface of the bedside cabinet. A book lay closed on its bookmark, barely dipped into.

Alice considered the contents of her room - did they represent the true values of her life - the most precious? Was there nothing better to look forward to? The boys she used to dream about in that bed, the hugging of crushed pillows, the furious scrawl in her diary, the salt tears that matted her lashes.

Her father, Alan, often went to the Horse and Jockey during the week - he was missing his drinking partner, Andy, who was apparently still cavorting around Europe. Simon and David sometimes popped in for a quick lager before heading off to some unknown venue in town.

She decided this Wednesday would be as good as any.

She would resolve it once and for all - it wasn't closure she was after, it was a new beginning.

CHAPTER NINETEEN

Alice twisted a lock of hair over one eye, but decided that was going too far. She applied a new lipstick - a racy pink - pinched her cheeks, and tugged mascara through her lashes. Was this a bit much for a mid week drink? Perfume was dabbed on wrists and behind ears. Her skirt was reasonably short and showed off her legs but not too much of them. She matched this with a smart white top that glittered like mica. A short black jacket was finally chosen with a thick belt, which was left unbuckled and hanging loose. A purse was dropped in a marginally larger handbag and clicked shut.

She was thinking about David - you're the one that I want.

(Ooh, ooh, ooh - said Inner Voice - he's far too young for you).

Alice ignored Inner Voice. At one time she'd even tried giving this voice a more empathetic identity, one she could work with but it remained 'Inner Voice,' and lately it had been a right bastard.

Maybe David would be one of those people who quickly aged - one day looking fresh-faced and youthful, the next drawn and lined. As they grew older together, the age gap wouldn't be an issue anyway - it would become less and less noticeable.

"You look nice, Alice."

Or perhaps David would have a dreadful experience, an ordeal that would age him. It happens to some people - those who lose loved ones or witness terrible events. It had happened to Jackie from the office who lost her husband Karl to cancer a few years ago. The weight fell off her and her face became a blank - scoured of expression. Jackie seemed to age about ten years overnight and her hair, usually dyed the jettest of blacks, lost its colour and composure, and fell listlessly about her face.

(Sublimation through consolation - said Inner Voice - is all you can ever hope for).

"Sorry?" said Alice.

"I said you look nice."

Her mother shuffled past, smiling at her daughter's reflection in the mirror.

Alice produced a twitching pink tissue from her handbag and dabbed at her cheek, squishing down an imaginary speck of dirt.

Her mother smiled. She was pleased that Alice was making an extra special effort for Michael Maddox - he was a good catch.

The traffic was slowly building up, and James Jones shifted his weight on the low brick wall, curling his lip into its very best sneer.

"Just look at them two tossers!"

"Fuckin' wankers."

Both of the James's were perched on the wall, aimlessly watching the early evening turnaround, their listless attention fixed on David and Simon who were walking down the street towards the Horse and Jockey.

Earlier, the two James's had watched a Ford Capri, heavily

dented, stop to let an old man cross. The man had slowly shuffled across the road, his open mouth slack and ghoulish. The driver of the car revved the engine, but the old man continued walking slowly, causing the traffic behind to sound their horns or shout abuse. In the end, the cars didn't wait for the old man to step up onto the kerb but swerved around him.

"Miserable old fucker," said the other James.

"Isn't that one of the slags from the college?" said James Jones nodding in the direction of Alice who came scuttling along the other side of the road, her too-tight skirt impeding the flow of her legs.

One of the straps on her shoes had come undone and was spinning at the heel.

"What are we doing here anyway?" said the other James, now bored with the aimless watching thing.

"What else is there to do - you got homework or something?"

"Fuck that."

He was holding a polished stone plucked from the ground, and was spinning it around in his hand. It was glossy, warm and a rich brown, like a conker ripped fresh from its spiky husk.

"This stone's just like a conker," he said.

He enjoyed the feel of it, rolling it around in his hand, and tossing it up into the air to catch with his other hand.

"If you soak them in vinegar," said the other James, "conkers go rock hard."

James Jones watched a couple of packed coaches drive past, followed by a few taxis, and then several cars with football scarves hanging out of the windows.

His attention was suddenly caught by two figures approaching the pub from the other side of the road.

"Ashley Stape used to cook his conkers in the oven to make them go even harder."

One of the figures was Maddox. Even from where he was

sitting, James Jones could see the man's lips slightly parted -
he imagined his nostrils and eyes widening too as though
scenting a quarry.

There was a wolfish feint to this strange lecturer, it was a
language of its own, and - there! - the glint of a canine,
bone-white, fracturing his grin. And the way he walked,
compared to his companion who, Jones was surprised to
see was none other that the new teacher, Turdy Snodgrass,
was pure wolf - easy and measured, self-contained and
assured.

A small crowd appeared around the corner composed
mainly of young men eating hot dogs with ketchup; a few
older men and the occasional girl or woman mingled within,
wrapped up and scarfed to the hilt. There was a lot of
shouting and chanting as the crowd moved rapidly along
the street past the pub.

"Villa must be playing tonight," said the other James.

"Fucking hate football, me!"

James Jones saw Turdy Snodgrass look up and take in the
moving crowd - Maddox hardly seemed to notice but
stepped to one side and ushered the other man into the
pub.

Some of the crowd peeled off and headed back to the pub,
keen to get a last one in before kick-off. The old man had
reappeared and could be seen slowly shuffling back across
the road, already the traffic backing up behind him.

Someone was talking to her father when Alice entered the
pub - a thin, wispy man of middle age, wearing a white shirt
and trousers, and the air of an office worker or sales rep.
He was venting his fury on something or other with
flustering, emotive grimaces, his eyeballs aching in their
sockets.

Who is he? She thought.

But, before that, Alice's first thought had been: where's
David?

When David did loom into view, carrying a couple of pints of lager in his hands, and a packet of cheese and onion crisps gripped in his teeth, a tiny fizz of lust detonated within her.

David was wearing his torn jeans and the faded brown tee shirt, which had tiny rips in the sleeves. It seemed such a daft fashion and yet it suited him perfectly. Alice wondered if she could carry it off too but that wasn't daft - just plain, bloody stupid. She didn't need Inner Voice to tell her this.

When Maddox came through the door, she tried to stir the little sherbet bombs of fizzing glee within her but there was nothing doing.

She was pleased to see him but not inordinately pleased. An excessive reaction was what she courted - a little fish that flipped in the stomach, a tightening of the throat that staunched words - something to dilate her pupils.

These are the natural reactions to extreme attraction, thought Alice. But how necessary were these sudden searing jolts to her future happiness - the tumbling, shaking bursts that would fetch up under her rib cage every time David grazed her with a look - his sunburst smile, his open, earnest face.

Alice knew, absolutely knew without any doubt, that it would never be the same with Maddox but would that be such a bad thing? Despite herself, she did not always welcome the random pummellings, which twisted her insides, and left her wrung out and pegged up to dry.

The best option was always the safest choice, but it was her self-proclaimed day of reckoning - and if the opportunity presented itself, the least she could do was try to take it.

Thin, wispy man was now whingeing to her father about students, calling into question their unsavoury appetites, their disregard for personal spaces. He endorsed this diatribe with examples and illustrations of their misbehaviour - many of these involving traffic cones and all night parties.

"Really?" said Maddox, putting a tray of drinks down on the table. "For my own part, I generally find students agreeably vital and brutish - an exhilarating combination."

They all stood around one of the tables except for Alan and wispy man who were perched on high stools.

David collected a couple of stools from around the bar - the pub was gradually emptying as supporters left for the football match. Snodgrass, who had hardly said a word, seemed a little edgy and gulped at his pint.

She wandered over to the bar and found a stool for herself, carrying it over and pulling it close to the boys.

Alice sat entranced by wispy man's expression - one of distaste but with conviction crumbling into tacit agreement with Maddox. Was it really that easy for Maddox to hold strangers in his thrall? It wasn't long before wispy man's aching eyes alighted on someone across the pub, and he excused himself.

Alan was glad to see wispy man go and said as much. "He's OK in small doses but he does go on a bit."

"Who is he anyway?" asked Alice taking a sip of her drink, and leaning across the table as though she was particularly keen to learn this information.

"Someone who used to know Andy. He hasn't seen him for months now either."

"Andy?" Maddox raised an eyebrow. "Wasn't he the chap here last time? A friend of yours, Alan - a gardener, I seem to remember - or a painter and decorator perhaps?"

"A landscape gardener," said Alice, leaning back, just a little closer to David. "He hasn't been seen since that night we were all here - disappeared off the face of the earth. Even the police are looking for him."

"I wonder," said Maddox. "Perhaps he's gone the same way as Gill Preston."

"Who?" said Alan.

"A former member of staff," said Snodgrass. "I was offered the vacancy after she left to go travelling in Brazil."

"Bolivia."

"He was always talking of travelling but there was a huge gulf between what he said and what he did." Alan held his arms wide apart as if measuring an imaginary fish.

At first, Alan had been miffed at not being privy to his best friend's plans - he especially missed his Friday Night Specials when they would get wasted. After their last session, he had woken up with his head in a pizza box. Jean had given him terrible stick but it was true what she had said - he was getting too old for this caper - leave the late nights to the youngsters and act your age.

Simon and David exchanged wintry looks of complicity and smiled knowingly before leaving the table. Was it possible, Alice wondered, that they knew about Andy trying to press his boner against her that night at the bar?

"Maybe he changed his identity," said Snodgrass, who had remained largely silent throughout the evening.

Alice wondered why Maddox had brought him along in the first place.

"Perhaps he had plastic surgery or an extreme make over. It's easily done these days."

"Indeed," said Maddox. "Perhaps he had a face lift."

Alice looked around and wondered where David and Simon had suddenly gone - the beer garden probably so Simon could have a crafty fag.

Outside the pub, traffic was backed up into a long line of trembling, choking vehicles. She heard someone shout: "Will someone shoot that fucking old cunt before I run him over!"

Snodgrass was soon on his fourth pint and tucking into some pork scratchings. He sidled over to Alice. Alan and Maddox were deep in conversation, and there was still no sign of David and Simon - how long does it take to smoke a cigarette for God's sake!

"Are you married?" Snodgrass's question was unexpected, and came with a blast of porky rind breath.

"No, I'm not married - I don't do relationships," she paused, wondering if she had coined this phrase herself or heard it from someone else.

Alice looked at him with wide and cautious eyes.

"Are you?"

"No, still looking for the one."

There was an uncomfortable pause, then:

"I'm just going to find my brother."

She looked towards the door leading out to the beer garden. Perhaps now was a good time to engage David. Alice excused herself and stepped down off her stool. Snodgrass shrugged four pints worth of shrug as if to signify that it wasn't for him to grant permission.

She made for the ladies' toilets to put her appearance to rights as best she could, bringing forth the new lipstick and applying a fresh sheen. If she let David know today how she felt - or perhaps how she'd been feeling, then something would be put into place that couldn't be undone. To be able to move on, to have verification for her emotional investment, she needed to know if this particular lock could be tumbled - if a beautiful world waited on the other side of a shuttered room. All evening, Alice tried to gauge the right moment to talk to him alone - maybe now was as good a time as any if Simon could be coaxed away for a short while.

She'd had a couple of gin and tonics because it was best not to be too clear-headed on this one - always best to leave a little drunken escape clause if it all became too awkward.

Alice held the door open but couldn't see them in the gathering dusk so she strolled out onto the deserted patio, stepping over discarded cigarette butts and the occasional gob of spit. Moths flitted around the lit windows, and gauzy fountains of gnats spurted above the patio lamps. There was no one around. The edge of the beer garden was screened behind some empty beer barrels and three large industrial dustbins. A black cat slunk out from under a bin and padded out in front of her. Was she destined to be lucky? A weathered trellis with curls of crisp dead leaves still attached to the wooden struts had been leant up against the near wall. Alice was sure she could hear a muffled sound - a stifled murmuring beyond the arc of the patio lights. Moving beyond the pool of light, her eyes growing accustomed to the murky backdrop, she looked through the intervening spaces in the wooden framework.

For a few seconds, which seemed to fill the night, she watched as the brown tee-shirt strained tightly across David's back as he held Simon - their chests pressed tightly together as they hungrily sought each others' mouths.

PART TWO

CHAPTER TWENTY

Was it really such a short time since the collapse of their wedding?

It was all a bit of a blur. Did they call off the reception? Alice couldn't remember - she was certain they tried to cancel the meal but it was too short notice. Her father had spent a couple of fruitless hours searching for Maddox - he had driven all over the place, even going so far as the golf course on the edge of town, and the woods behind the cemetery.

Her father said he wanted to punch Maddox - smack him one. There was a complaint from her mother about all the guests drinking the wine even though the wedding hadn't gone ahead but Alice was past caring.

Toby Szubanski had finished off two bottles of red himself, and was seen walking out with another bottle. The cake had been cut into moist wedges and handed around but the presents had to be sent back. Her mother said that

Mrs Postans had collected up all the little lace doilies and ribbon-wrapped favours because her son, Matthew, was getting married next year, and they would come in handy.

Was it really such a short time when everything in her world suddenly shattered, and all the pieces that needed picking up were kicked out of sight? Funny how things turn out - the devastation she felt afterwards took her by surprise, given the somewhat ambiguous feelings she had leading up to the wedding.

Even as the big day approached, Alice remembered thinking that if David said it was all just one big mistake - him and Simon - that they had been drunk, and were just fooling around, she would have dropped Maddox like the proverbial.

Hypocrisy - double standards? Sure, but Alice did have a genuine regard for Maddox, a fondness and affection she was convinced would suffice. She could picture the two of them in a tender embrace, a guarded proximity that excluded others but invited approval nevertheless. She certainly had her mother's blessing - and everyone had been very much in favour. Was this all she needed to prop up her life? But it wasn't what she really wanted - that blissful ignorance she once scorned would have put her in a much better place than she was now.

That blissful ignorance ended a long time ago when she had seen her beloved David snogging the face off Simon - when the unrequited became the unrequitable.

She eventually returned to her small Bournville flat, and sat by the upstairs window looking out across the village green. It was a perfectly miserable day, maudlin and dreary, the low sky a greasy grey with a weak sun hardly troubling it. Shivery raindrops wiggled down the windowpane.

Alice unpeeled the lid off a small tub of ice cream, and wistfully poked the little wooden spoon into its contents, giving them a slow stir. She missed this, the comfortable sadness - the lonely grief of her thoughts.

The lamp in her bedroom threw out a sharp yellow light, giving a sallow cast to her features; she blew out a long sigh of resignation - her signature tune.

There was a man outside, walking across the green, carrying groceries in a couple of plastic carrier bags. He seemed oblivious to the fact that one of the bags was ripped, and a thin line of oats or cereal trailed behind him. The man continued walking towards a small band of shops that edged the green, spilling his wares as he went.

Something had spilled inside her too.

Her eyes followed the man all along the green until he stopped and sat on a bench. Against the recently painted vivid green of the bench, his coat seemed marked and oily. Discovering the seepage, he lifted the leaky carrier bag up to eye-level, spinning it to locate the slit. A few more grains spilled out and tumbled at his feet.

Tears brimmed in her eyes. If only emotional turmoil wasn't so damned exhausting. Surely it had been for the best they hadn't married in the end. Better that he had spurned her, (ditched her at the altar more like). The anguish and collapse of all she held dear - the folding in on itself of her manufactured dream - had totally wrung her out, like a twisted bed sheet - scorched and plaited with fever.

Hurt, humbled and humiliated - there was no bewitched, bothered and bewildered about it - Alice had been truly stunned when Maddox turned on his heel and walked out of the church.

She had been crushed, but it had been nothing like the boning she felt when her eyes had fallen on David and Simon. All sense of reality had been jammed out of her, as if bands of steel had corseted her and bound their spirals tight across her chest - her brother pinned to the wall by David in a scalding embrace that Alice had dreamed about night after night for herself.

Maddox hadn't really noticed at the time but David did have the most beguiling eyes.

It was a thought that struck him as he unrolled Andy's face, and laid it against Gill's to compare and contrast the different textures.

Andy's eyeless lids had bedded down in the parchment of the skin, gently curling up at the edges - there was little protrusion to speak of. He brushed a rime of frost from Gill's stricken face - he would need some boiled water, and some nifty scalpel work to prise it off if he decided on a fresh new one. That was the trouble with death - it did crinkle so.

If the eyes could be isolated soon, they would bed down sufficiently well in the clammy sockets of the face. The unforgiving resin mix of the laboratory skull might push the eyes out in startled pop-ups if he didn't thumb them down. Hopefully fresh ones would be more malleable. Alternatively, he could gouge out shallow depressions in the resin so the eyeballs would nest more realistically. So much to do, so little time.

Time was pressing; he regretted taking the honeymoon now, two whole weeks away when he could have been gathering valuable new material for his work.

The wedding had been a mistake, especially at such short notice. He was sorry that he had walked out on Alice - she didn't deserve that. However, Maddox was a creature, not of habit or even impulse, but a creature of disconnection. There was a clinical detachment to his actions - an innate core that never responded to consequences in anything other than a precise, dissociated way.

Her father, Alan, had punched him - punched him twice. He had walked into the Horse and Jockey and punched Maddox to the floor, so enraged had he been. Maddox had been affronted by the attack. He hadn't been afraid - primal instincts withdrew in an instant - sifted and stored in his mind.

Instantly accessible, he would locate this file in time and address it. It was in a file labeled 'unfinished business' and 'loose ends' - a particularly slim file. There was little about Maddox that could ever be considered unfinished or loose - just pending.

The exhibition, he had been informed, was only a matter of months away. Perhaps a liver wouldn't go amiss now - or a few coils of intestine. Looking into the freezer, the overall effect of his work was generally pleasing but the face and hair remained a problem.

Anyone viewing his work would naturally begin at the head before appraising the rest of the unit. It would be the face that would grab them - or the sprung ribs perhaps.

The ribs had been a great acquisition. Although reasonably happy with the torso he had procured, the ribs that originally came with it had been a little on the concave side. This produced a tendency to draw the sternum up into a pigeon chest - not the effect he was after. By pitting each rib with the smallest serration, and slicing short darts through the inter costal muscles, he was able to reduce the dome of the chest by placing a serving tray of bricks on the upper body, and letting it tamp down the flesh overnight.

Now that he had his own genuine article, Maddox was less anxious about discarding the classroom skeleton. It had been the perfect model on which to arrange his work, but was largely redundant now that his own skeletal framework was taking shape. Almost all of the requisite anatomy had been secured, and it had been easy to freeze and thaw the tissues as required, manipulating them to the bone, hitching each shard and tear of flesh to its attendant mooring.

In Birmingham there were many street people and beggars - mendicants on the margin of society - and each one harboured a body as disposable as razor blades or tampons. Occasionally, one or two of them could be found gathered together in the quietest recesses of the canal network, under bridges or clustered around old, disused railway sidings.

Here they would congregate - smoking stunted cigarettes and downing strong cider before eventually moving on into the city centre.

They were a readily available source of fleshy revenue that Maddox had been loathe to tap into at first, but with time being constrained, he felled a couple of likely tramps under a disused railway bridge.

This short adjunct to the main waterway was his own personal favourite stretch of the canal, and he would sometimes take a stroll from the campus to the city centre along the towpath. In the cold mornings, it was particularly attractive with hoar frost crackling underfoot, and the dun bracken braided with furry ice. Woody vegetation alongside the bridge was thick, glued together with the cracked windscreens of frosted spider webs.

Maddox used a cudgel to brain the two tramps - one after the other, their gin-sodden eyes and rotted-stump maws barely flickered as they keeled over, sunken dents mushed in the side of their heads.

The tramps had emerged from underneath an old, crumbling bridge - a remnant from an ancient rail track that ran parallel to the canal, screened by wire fencing and keep-out signs. Bricked up at the furthest end, it provided a tight shelter against wind and rain.

Killing the old, worn men had been like dispatching the dead - they were drunk and dithery even before he struck them, and Maddox missed the delicious little frisson he always experienced before a kill - the split-second of alarm that fleetingly ignited in terrified eyes. He resented being deprived of it.

Maddox slipped the cudgel back into his rucksack, and looked along the towpath for any errant joggers and cyclists but it was all deathly quiet.

There was another man under the bridge who Maddox hadn't noticed at first. It was the gurgle of sodden sleep that alerted him to a bleary form, sprawled out beneath gnawed cardboard boxes and a pile of damp blankets.

The sleeping man, a teenager really, was clad in a dirty white tracksuit with an equally grubby baseball cap pulled over his eyes. Maddox flicked at the boy's face with his long, bony fingers but the lad remained unconscious, gurgling gently in his sweet oblivion.

More empty bottles and a few crushed cans of Special Brew were spread around the ground. Plastic bags lay steamed up beside an old wooden crate - the smell of glue was rank on the boy. Maddox felt the span of ribs under the grimy tee shirt, pressing down gently with his long hands to assess the curve and spring of the bones.

Maddox regretted killing the other two men for there would be little to salvage from their bodies that wasn't corrupted or damaged in some way - a scarred liver and mottled kidney would be of no use to him whatsoever.

With his foot, Maddox nudged one of the bodies of the felled men. It was like prodding a thin wet sack; there was an underlying sense of wasted and brittle life - of honeycombed bone and fruit flesh, like the frozen soldiers on blasted battlefields - scarified and clutching at the cold white air.

There was no weight to either of the wasted bodies, and Maddox effortlessly dragged the first of the corpses into the undergrowth, intending to go back later that night, and carry both of them over to the canal bridge. From the top of the bridge, he would hoist them over the wall and let them drop into the thick vegetation on the other side of the embankment. There wasn't a towpath on the opposite side, and both bodies would sink from view under the thick matted ivy and weeds that clothed the banks. No doubt they would smell for a short while but it was unlikely anyone would bother looking for someone not missing. No one would be stirred by the absence of nameless vagrants.

Nettles spiked the red ground at the den entrance where grey splintered beams rotted and meshed with the earth.

Twisted flaking girders spanned shallow pits of yellow rainwater where black insects skittered across the surface.

A disturbed cat, ginger or strawberry blonde - Maddox wasn't sure - left off its foraging and slunk back into the shadows.

Maddox tapped at the other corpse with his foot.

"Who are you...what are you doing?" Grubby Tracksuit's voice had a trembling, croaky timbre, raw from cigarettes, glue and alcohol. He was standing, almost crouching, beneath the lower arc of the bridge like a fragile lemur caught in a hunter's sights.

"Oh you know, nothing much. Having a bit of a walk."

Maddox pulled the second corpse into the undergrowth, and pushed a wayward limb under some nettles with his foot.

"What did you do to them?" Grubby Tracksuit held onto the walls as he inched his way along the damp brickwork, not quite bold enough to leave the sanctuary of his haven, or brave enough to stand his corner. His lips were broken and sore, tiny pewter veins threaded their way up either side of his nose.

Maddox reached for his rucksack, and began fumbling around inside it.

"Is he asleep - did you kill him? Where's Paddy?" Grubby Tracksuit's voice was cracking a bit now - a little gulpy.

"So many questions."

Grubby Tracksuit eventually emerged from the darkness, squinting into the watery light. He held his hands out in supplication - the fingernails were chewed to the quick. They would have been no use whatsoever.

His eyes were rimmed raw, trimmed with an almost luminescent blood red. The boy was slim in build, but the chest was good, ribs bellowing to the rapid beats of his heart.

Maddox could see that he was breathing heavily now, struggling to control his anxiety. The boy kept touching his face and sniffing, running the heel of his hand along the side of his face, and snatching at his hair.

"Classic displacement activity," said Maddox.

"I don't mean no harm."

"How very reassuring."

Some rusted iron tables were scattered on the ground in front of the bridge, the skeletal remains of a mattress flopped against one of them. A little wren, brown as a farthing, whirred out of a hole in the brickwork.

Grubby Tracksuit peered back into the shadowy bridge - a nervous little rodent out of its hole.

"I ain't done nothing, you can't keep me here."

The boy's voice was shrill - a little vexed.

Maddox delved deeper into his rucksack.

He was quite young - a callow youth - pinched cheeks, doughy skin blistered with boils around the ears - brooding, broken mouth, colourless lids.

"Ah, here we are."

Maddox's hand gripped onto a handle.

The boy's eyes were wide with terror.

"What are you doing with that mache..."

Maddox had been here before.

One of Grubby Tracksuit's eyes had a slight cast to it, the merest suggestion of a droopy eyelid or a lazy eye - it was difficult to tell - especially now with the head not being attached to the neck any more. The new machete that Maddox had purchased was a supreme beast, and possessed perfect heft and balance.

The cervical vertebrae had popped cleanly once he'd delivered the cut, and the boy's head had spun from his neck, bouncing over a couple of rotten sleepers before gazing up with boss-eyed astonishment.

CHAPTER TWENTY-ONE

When Alice bumped into Maddox for the first time since their aborted wedding, he was carrying a small cardboard box containing some photocopied handouts, a clipboard, and several pens - the pens held fast by a thick rubber band. A little bruising to the cheek lightly marked his face, as if someone had punched him.

She had known he was back at the college - his black Ford Focus was parked in a spot outside the main college entrance.

He walked into the staff room where Alice was making herself a mug of tea. The strap on her sandal had come loose, and she'd had to clench her toes to stop it slapping along the corridor. She was looking forward to a good sit down.

"Hello Alice."

"Oh, it's you."

"Yes, how are you?"

This was a scene that had continually spooled through her mind since that horrendous day, and racked up at the back of her mind was a whole tier of retorts and reactions, a litany of cutting ripostes and blistering broadsides. Scorned Alice had hell-bent fury at the ready - richly funded with lacerating comebacks and ill-concealed contempt - and it was on Michael Maddox's moral destruction that she was wholly bent.

"I'm good," she said.

"I feel I must apologise - my behaviour was inexcusable, quite reprehensible in the circumstances."

"That's putting it mildly."

"If you think there may be something I can do to make amends, please don't hesitate to ask."

Maddox was relaxed, not even the slightest catch to his voice. He jostled the cardboard box a little, and placed it on the counter.

"I'll live."

A pause - and then:

"Of course, you will."

Maddox nudged the roll of pens to an edge of the box so that they sat neatly in the corner.

"May I trouble you to return my spare keys when you get the chance?"

And with that, he left the staff room.

The nerve of the man! As well as his spare keys, Alice still had a few bits and pieces belonging to him, including a couple of books. She would rail against his possessions - it was all she had left.

Already Alice was compiling an imaginary note to lash to his belongings: 'Good Riddance to Bad Rubbish' was as clichéd as it came, but she could almost feel the fat marker pen hot in her hand as she gouged out the message.

Returning to the office, Alice slumped down in a chair next to Val, who was eating a chocolate éclair and flicking through a sheath of documents. She glanced up from her reading, and then held one of the pages out at arm's length as if suddenly realising her eyes were better at this distance.

On a cork notice board above their heads, there was a

general office invite to Sandra's flat-warming party - Bring a Bottle and a Fella! it said in lurid lime-green highlighter.

"You OK?" asked Val.

"Fine."

"You sure?"

"Please don't go on - it isn't necessary to keep reassuring me - I just need to be left alone."

"Well, you came over to me," said Val, with a slight hint of miff. She pulled herself up from behind the desk. "I could have checked these printouts tomorrow morning - I didn't need to do them today."

Val's top had a high neck to it but a few folds of flesh threatened to overflow - she grabbed the printouts and, licking a fat finger, stabbed at a few stray pastry crumbs, her lips smacking at the taste.

Well, that went rather well, thought Maddox, as he made his way to the creative writing class. He was due to observe the session, and appraise Snodgrass who, after an unsteady start, was making good progress on the module.

"Excuse me," Maddox said as he quietly opened the door and took a seat at the back of the room. The two James's were huddled together in the back row. James Jones sat up a tad straighter - the other James continued with his slump.

"Why what you done?" said the other James, looking around and grinning at James Jones.

"May I?" asked Maddox, reaching over and taking a book from one of the students in front of him. "Do you mind sharing? Only I've forgotten to bring a copy."

Maddox took out a note pad, and checked the lesson plan attached to his clipboard. He watched as Snodgrass began to discuss the use of similes and metaphors in creative writing.

Maddox was surprised at the confidence and ease of his delivery.

"When learning to use similes and metaphors," Snodgrass

began, his voice clear and confident, "it is the subtle use of these literary devices, which often carry the most weight."

Maddox scrolled down his checklist and came to a box marked 'Voice Projection' and ticked it with a red pen. He jotted a few favourable comments regarding pace and diction, and looked up with an expression, which could almost have been described as beatific if it wasn't for the prominent eyetooth pulling a dent across his faint smile.

"However, in some cases," Snodgrass continued, "similes are inappropriate to the natural flow of a sentence - the scenario being conveyed in a passage of writing can be considerably enhanced by using metaphors instead."

Maddox ticked another box.

"Remember that in many cases, less is more - less is more!" he repeated like a song thrush at the end of a summer storm.

It was an impressive performance - Maddox approved of the quaint rituals Snodgrass performed to maintain his composure - pulling out little props from the drawer of his desk, or from a box on the front table to illustrate a point.

Peering into the box on the table, Snodgrass clutched his chin, and appeared deep in thought as if wondering where on earth he was before suddenly coming to. He took out a blue silk scarf from the drawer.

"This isn't mine," he joked, the awkward smile desperately beckoning others to join it. "Although this is a scarf - a simple blue scarf, it would be quite acceptable to say something was scarfed with something else - or in something else. That would be an example of a metaphor."

Maddox wrote: 'Poor example for explaining metaphors!'

"Is 'scarfed' a proper word, sir?" asked one of the students in the front row, a pale freckled thing with a prominent overbite.

"Yes, I'm sure it is."

"What would be scarfed with something sir - necks?"

"Well, yes, I suppose it could be used for necks, if used

173

collectively, and referring to a crowd of people perhaps. I was thinking more of a tree, its branches being scarfed with fruit, or a low field scarfed with early morning mist. Of course, if you said the mist in the early morning was like a scarf, that would be a simile."

"Isn't it easier to say a lot of people with a lot of scarfs?"

"This is why you would use it as an effective metaphor - much smoother than a mere literal description."

"If some of the people didn't wear scarfs, they wouldn't all be scarfed though. You couldn't say they were scarfed if some of them weren't wearing scarfs."

"The point is..." Snodgrass said, a slight splinter of exasperation spiking his voice. "The point is the usage of the word - the way it can be utilised as metaphor. There are many words in the English language which transfer easily into metaphors - these make the sentences pop, they make the language come alive!"

Snodgrass then took a knife out of the box, and began to feel its edge, and the sharp tip - it was slightly curved, and glinted steely under the lights as he turned it slowly in his hand. Maddox thought this kind of knife would require a good upward thrust, followed by a twist if it was ever to exact some penance. However, there were no obvious serrations and the blade would pull free smoothly.

Snodgrass demonstrated a stabbing motion, like a Zulu with an assegai perhaps. The two James's sat up, the lesson suddenly becoming interesting.

"A knife through the heart? Now this would be a literal description if outlining the actual stabbing, the act of someone being attacked or assaulted. However, metaphorically, it could be used to describe an emotional wounding - a heartbreak."

"Isn't 'heartbreak' a metaphor too, sir?" said Overbite who would soon lose his front teeth to a particularly savage attack by James Jones later that month.

"That's correct. Also the expression 'cuts like a knife' is a classic simile. Then we have the mixed metaphor..."

"What a load of old bollocking shite," said the other James.

James Jones had just about enough of the other James. It wasn't just his pithy and childish comments - he himself rejoiced in such flippancy - but his best friend had come to represent certain aspects about himself that he found difficult to embrace lately.

Jones felt that he had now moved through the murky morass of adolescence - a startling development that no longer welcomed the puerile, but was moving towards darker, more rounded territory. In short, he wanted to be like Maddox.

He wanted to pulsate with the finely distilled evil he had detected in the lecturer - it rippled off the man, and yet everyone interpreted it as charisma. Or was he, James Jones, some kind of latent familiar able to tap into such energy? The thought thrilled him. Maddox had great presence but Jones could only see an absence - there was a dereliction of all things good - an instinct rather than a trait, one that absolved the bearer of any inequity.

James Jones coveted just such a gift. He was tired of juvenilia and felt it was time to put away childish things. He decided the other James was simply another childish thing to put away.

"Let's go and stone the ducks in the park," suggested the other James.

The park was one of their favourite haunts, a mustering place after school - preferable to the precinct, which was so passé these days.

They had spent many summer evenings throwing stones at the ducks and swans on the lake. They never killed any of the huge white birds but simply drove them off into deeper water. The birds would hiss and bluster and, if Jones was truthful, he was a little scared of them.

Everywhere and everything was boring, and there was

175

nothing on television - although he would always try to watch Coronation Street if no one was around to see him do so.

Shoplifting had lost its edge. Security tags could be a problem so they targeted smaller shops and stores, avoiding the major retailers.

Often they ended up with worthless tat - one foray yielded a roll of dark purple ribbon and a jar of whole-grain mustard — another had secured two plastic mugs with kittens on.

As for girls - they were the eternal conundrum, and Jones was reluctant to compete for any girl's affection if the other James was around.

Whereas he was clunky and wide-mouthed, the other James was smiley cute, and slim as an otter. Some of the girls would talk to the other James, and Jones would dress up his simmering envy with chilly indifference.

Both of the James's lived in opulent surroundings on the Four Oaks estate, wanting for nothing but needing everything - boredom the bane of their short lives.

Soon he would be old enough to experiment with drugs, but these too, along with swans, frightened him.

At night, he fell asleep contented but not knowing why, enjoying the fantasies and dreams, which rarely involved comely girls, but instead laid down sweet expectations of another life yet to be claimed.

This other life would include more than the vapid trappings of a middle class existence, and would be forged from something different entirely.

Not for him the selfless awakenings of a life given to pleasure - or the better good. He wanted the better bad, and the figure of Maddox loomed large in his thoughts - a mentor rather than a lecturer.

Alice felt unsettled and a little jumpy after seeing Maddox again, and was grateful now for Val's company.

Even now, she thought - even now after what he has put me through - humiliation hardly featured at all. There had been the earlier shunning of friends and colleagues, of course - lest any word of consolation be uttered - any snug phrases ventured that should fit the occasion.

But the simple truth was that Alice had liked Maddox well enough - but not quite well enough.

After the wedding, and the nights that followed, gobbets of vitriol glued thoughts to the roof of her skull where they lay trapped and broiled in indignation. Always bumping, like wasps at a car window, they were difficult to dislodge. But there was always a consoling glimmer of relief - a little shard of liberation - in forsaking the martyrdom of her marriage to someone she didn't love for the continual devotion to someone she could never have.

She apologised to Val for being 'a bit off' with her, and promised to buy her lunch at the weekend.

On the way home, she passed St Gregory's churchyard, and felt obliged to kindle a pained expression - the whisper of a shudder that would pay an appropriate tithe to her abandonment. But instead, like a series of short rabbit punches to the kidneys, it was those defining shots of Simon and David together that pummelled her.

It was these memories that snapped at her whenever she passed the Horse and Jockey, with its conspiratorial beer garden.

As a teenager, Alice had enjoyed reading the popular magazines, especially the problem pages, relishing the features on unrequited love, and yearned to garner some of these intense emotions in her own life. Alice had insisted that such a rite of passage was her due, and looked forward to wallowing in it, for what young teenage girl would not want to subject herself to such a convenient pool of misery.

In the end, Alice simply felt gutted.

She wouldn't be the only one.

CHAPTER TWENTY-TWO

The dogs were starving.

They had not been fed.

Occasionally a dry hoarse whimper would flutter from their muzzles but instinctively they knew better than to growl or bark or snarl. Knew better than to raise their hackles, or bare teeth or curl lips.

Conditioning was as glaringly evident in these animals as it ever was in Pavlov's dogs - the wreckage of their teased minds too ravaged to pitch their whines any higher lest Maddox repeat the punishment that had cowed them in the first place.

But that didn't stop them panging with hunger, or salivating over the faintest waft of a mouth-watering aroma.

Binky was slavering, his muzzle limed with thick ropes of saliva as he chomped down on the single dog biscuit spun to him over the steel pen in the kitchen. The other dog - Maddox couldn't remember its name - frantically snaffled his thrown biscuit, bone-shaped and mealy, lest Binky snatch it from him. Binky was the top dog here, but only as far as the kitchen went.

Maddox looked around the kitchen. Jonathan Mortimer had given the whole place a good clean before leaving for the Lake District. The floor had been scrubbed - all surfaces wiped down, and the pots and pans gleamed. Potted cacti shone in their little terracotta beds on the window sill, and a bunch of ailing daffodils sat in a glass vase on the kitchen table. Twists of spotted flypaper spun from the ceiling.

The kitchen was much tidier than the last time he had been here - the day when Mortimer had been bitten by one of his own dogs.

Maddox opened the tins of dog food and poured out some dog biscuits, little bone shapes that clattered into plastic bowls. The empty tins and packets were piled up on the side of the sink, tantalising the dogs with heady, meaty aromas. The meat and biscuits were then scraped onto some spread newspapers and wrapped up in a bin-liner, ready to dispose of on his way home.

The dogs began to whine and salivate as the excruciating smell of jellies and marrows wafted through the kitchen. Binky's loose eyes shook in their sockets.

In the end, Jonathan Mortimer had been reluctant to ask Mrs Fenshaw to water the plants and feed the dogs. His frosty neighbour intimidated him with her sharp little glasses perched on an even sharper nose. Mrs Fenshaw had an abrupt manner, always checking the soles of her shoes when walking past Mortimer's house. He was more than happy to take up Maddox's offer to keep an eye on them while he was away - especially as Maddox decided he couldn't go to the Lakes after all.

Mortimer was disappointed with this last minute withdrawal - and wasn't particularly enamoured with Maddox suggesting Snodgrass be his replacement, but the rooms had been booked, and it seemed a waste to cancel at short notice.

Maddox turned on the tap, and let the cold water run a few more minutes before filling the water bowls. He leaned over the partition, taking care not to spill any water as he lowered the bowls onto the floor of the pen. There was hardly any poop to scoop as the dogs had been without food for sometime now. Binky risked a low growl but flinched when Maddox looked up and fixed him with a stare than would freeze a basilisk.

"I really don't fancy doing any rock climbing," Mortimer had said, packing his Kendal Mint Cake.

Mortimer had eventually driven off to the Lake District, leaving Maddox with the keys to the house, several cans of dog food and biscuits, some feeding instructions written down in red ink, and an insistence that he help himself to anything he fancied from the fridge.

Inside one of the cupboards, there was a bottle of port and another one of brandy - both slightly filmed with dust. The freezer was an uneconomical upright model, not much bigger than a large cardboard box - you certainly couldn't fit a body in there. Maddox swung the fridge door open and looked inside. It was stacked with food and, as he carefully took each item out, smiled to see they were all arranged by their sell-by dates.

Perhaps a piece of cheese and some port, he mused - before I begin.

In the next room, visible through the open door, Hawthorn James lay tethered and heavily sedated on a camp bed hardly a foot above the polished hardwood flooring, and well within spurting distance of the wipe-down, easy-to-clean leather furniture.

Earlier on that same day, with a hot sun shining and a cloudless blue sky hovering above the unmatched greenery of park and trees, James Jones braced himself for another punch.

Spring was moving quickly through the gears. In the late afternoon, the clean colours of the season were unfurled and dashed across lawns and gardens.

Maybe the teeth this time, Jones thought, they were rather prominent. He had deliberately picked on the freckled lad from his creative writing class after spotting him walking alone by the lake. Jones had been in a foul mood all day, and his hapless victim was ripe for a beating.

But even this assault seemed half-hearted - a mere cuffing behind some hedging - he couldn't find the other James anywhere to egg him on. Regardless of his recent vow to break up their friendship, and to somehow become an acolyte of Mr Maddox, Jones nevertheless constantly required an audience.

Along the far curving footpath that skirted the park, a couple of figures came into view, each with a walk so distinctive that Jones stiffened with outrage. Maddox and the other James were strolling along the far path, on the other side of the lake. What were they up to - what was his supposedly best mate, the other James, doing with Maddox? And, more importantly, what did the enigmatic lecturer want with his best friend?

James Jones wouldn't have believed it if he hadn't seen it with his own two eyes. He had been busily punching the teeth out of that ginger spotty-faced twat when these two figures suddenly popped up in the distance.

"Pweese," said Overbite as Jones gave him a last punch in the mouth. He was pretty sure the teeth had come out with that one.

Jones decided to follow them and see where they were heading - and it was with a strangely vague sense of betrayal that he set off. Yet the notion of disloyalty was alien to him. Did he feel spurned by Maddox - or by his friend? The unsettling form that this betrayal seemed to be taking was one he was unfamiliar with.

He had always hoped for some mutual recognition from Maddox - a kindling spark that may have pressed into orbit a fateful collaboration. Despite his uncertainty, there was still a gnawing insistence suggesting that he was on the

181

brink of some great thing - something almost preordained.

He had even asked Turdy Snodgrass a question about metaphors in the hope of catching Maddox's eye. What form this acknowledgement would take, he wasn't sure - only that he would know.

He stroked the grazed skin of his bruised knuckles as he watched them go.

Gently, with the latex of his rubber glove holding fast to the duodenum, Maddox began to tug the rest of the small intestine through the glistening cavity that gaped from Hawthorn James's elongated midriff.

There had been much snipping and clipping with the scissors, the mesenteries had been a bind, but now the long, steaming coils of the boy's intestines were being drawn slowly out, and draped in part over his bare arms. He needed both hands now, and the coils, slippery with mucus but pleasingly solid in weight, slithered and glooped around him.

"Wait!" he barked at the famished dogs as they wavered on the edge of the operating area, coarse matted coats staring, their clacking jaws spooled with saliva.

Released from their pen, they slowly retreated to the far side of the room, whining and scrabbling behind the leather sofa, but almost immediately began to inch forward again. Claws clacking on the hardwood floor, the dogs were drawn by the over-powering smell and ichorous delights that choked their senses and sent base, wanton instincts hurtling through them.

With his arms full, Maddox looked down at the surgical procedures printed out and arranged over the full length of the couch. The research undertaken proved very useful during the planning of the initial incisions; the material pulled from the Internet provided valid suggestions on harvesting internal organs. Bending down slightly so he could peruse the pages better, he read that, in humans, the intestine consisted of the small and large intestines - the small intestine being further divided into three major parts, which included the duodenum, the jejunum and the ileum.

He looked along the grisly bunting, which had unwound from the gaping maw of the opened torso, and tugged out a few more lengths of the purplish-grey coils. Maddox thought he had identified the duodenum, and held it fast in his gloved hand while pulling out another tumble of intestine. The fetid spirals clumped wetly to the hardwood floor, slapping against the polished grain.

Immediately one of the dogs was onto them, bolting down as much as he could with scrubbling, clackkity jaws.

Maddox barked at the dog, which quickly spun back behind the leather sofa, a slick wet panel of gut clasped in its teeth.

There was the oddly named jejunum, and he ticked one of the pages with the stub of a pencil, and the equally compelling ileum. Maddox ticked another page, but felt no inclination to include these in his work. The duodenum, he reckoned, would suffice and he ran his hands along its length, feeling the sliding ribs of muscle and tissue glide under his touch - the spongy tensile strength of the coils.

Digging deep with his long hands, fingers paddling in pockets of rich red blood, he pushed in further, forging a way through layers of loose tissue coated in mucus. Apparently, the whole slimy tract began at the pyloric sphincter of the stomach but even as Maddox bent down and leant in close to the blackening cavity, he couldn't recognise anything that looked like a sphincter.

He had inadvertently uncurled the section that curved around the head of the pancreas, and now lay on the right side of the anterior part of the abdomen. It was disappointing - he would have been interested in poking around in that.

Only a length of intestine would be required for his project - a representational strip - there was little point in including

183

the entire alimentary canal. Perhaps it would be best to limit himself to the duodenum and a few other compact segments - possibly snippets of the caecum and colon, which bore a fine rich, red colour.

All in all, he was quite pleased with the way things had gone. Hawthorn James had been effortlessly sedated after downing a large cocktail of port and brandy - nearly a full bottle. Ah, the bravado of youth!

The pills and injections kept him nicely under as Maddox slid his hand over the exposed belly, gently palpating the organs underneath the smooth skin. Then he used a long, bitter blade to slice him open from the base of his sternum to the pubis, neatly parting the skin so the layers of tissue and lick-clean muscle snapped into view. There were tough membranes to cut through before releasing the pulpy soft organs to his touch. Blood spattered onto the wooden floor - an alarmingly loud trickle, which pooled under his feet.

One of the dogs lapped at this puddled treat but Maddox shoed it away with his foot - certain standards had to be observed.

"What are you doing?" asked Hawthorn James.

"Oh, you're awake," said Maddox.

Before Hawthorn James's insides had been ripped out of him, he had been eager to follow Maddox from the park to Mr Mortimer's home - there were some textbooks and a few papers that needed collecting, and Mr Maddox would appreciate some help.

"I could use a hand if you're not too busy?"

A sneer rippled across Hawthorn James's upper lip.

"Fuck that!"

"Then perhaps I may ask Jones - is he around? He usually is."

It was not an opportunistic meeting. Maddox was well aware of the two James's regular haunts, which were limited and easy to narrow down. Some essential material was needed for his work, and stealth and caution would be deferred until this urgency was addressed.

Fortunately, neither of the James's were blessed with attentive parents - he calculated a good few days or so before any alarm would be raised. Soon, he could ship his work to the continent, and if he could stall proceedings over this one, he would need only the eyes and hair to complete the project.

Surprisingly, Hawthorn James was alone, out there on the edge of the park. Didn't the two James's come as a pair?

We're not joined at the hip, Hawthorn had replied, it's not as if I don't have my own life. He was having trouble maintaining the sneer, and allowed his lips to settle into a scornful pout.

Hawthorn James was quietly satisfied - he had become aware of James Jones's odd fascination for Maddox, and he looked to score some useful points over his friend who had been more than a little distant lately - a little too preoccupied.

Well, he could preoccupy this when he told him he'd been knocking around with his precious Mr Maddox. James Jones wasn't great at a lot of things, and trying to look calm and collected and not bothered when he was seething inside was just one of the many things he wasn't good at.

Hawthorn James had been quite looking forward to telling him.

"Not much else to do in this fucking dump," said Hawthorn, falling in behind Maddox.

The team-building event was scheduled halfway through the second semester. The whole venture was to be around Coniston Water, as strongly recommended by himself - and Gill, of course, before she left to find herself. Principal Richardson endorsed the trip, and there would be ample time between now and then to harvest all he needed for the exhibition. He would attend the first part of the week, dispose of a few odds and ends in the lake, and then leave for the exhibition. He had been sent the itinerary already, and all his travel and shipping arrangements could be made online.

Naturally, he would never be able to come back to England.

They had walked through the park, along the cinder path where lines of new saplings had been planted, their bases wrapped in rolled tubes of wire.

From the other side of the lake, James Jones seethed before losing them momentarily in the glare of sunlight through the trees. They then began to move beyond the gardens, and the busy playground where children squealed on rusty swings. From the park, it was a mere ten minute walk to Mortimer's house where Maddox had left the most delicious smelling joint of beef on the draining board. He could almost imagine the dogs going crazy with the hunger.

Hawthorn James had woken to a world of pain.

The last thing he remembered was walking back through the park with Mr Maddox who, and he wasn't exactly sure on this point, had somehow convinced him to walk back to someone's house - whose house? He seemed to think it belonged to one of the other lecturers but there was a gnawing pain at his stomach, which kept shaking his memories loose and jumbling them up. There was also a vague recollection of him gleefully agreeing but why - was there an opportunity for trouble involved, perhaps some extra curricular mayhem to indulge in? He couldn't remember if his best friend, James Jones, was involved in some way. It would be natural to assume his friend was, but he seemed to think - ouch!

"Sorry," said Maddox. "Bad dog!"

There was a dog tugging on what looked like a piece of his gut, a livid purplish tendril that looked ready to snap. Was that his intestine! Hawthorn James groaned, and every sensation in his body was suddenly yanked into a tight knot of agony. He tried lifting his head but was brought up short by another searing jolt of pain, a burning agony as ichorous fluids and liquids leaked into a succession of pits and wells.

His head burned, the whole scenario seemed surreal - was he alive? Was that really a dog eating his insides? With great effort, Hawthorn James craned his head and squinted down the length of his pale naked body. The dog seemed to be yanking hard on what seemed to be an elastic strip of his gut, and then, all of a sudden, there was another dog jostling for position around the pulp of his raw, open stomach. They both had their thick, heavy muzzles buried deep in his midriff, yammering and jostling, choking back their growls.

Maddox administered another injection. The boy's wrists were bound above his head and his ankles strapped somewhere out of sight, and all around him he was aware of a sickening, sweet stench - a floundering sickly smell. Ceiling lights cauterised his brain as he began to lose consciousness, ebbing and flowing between two worlds, his head banging as if a couple of chisels had been driven into his skull.

His mouth was dry, his lips cracked and his thirst was unbearable. There was only enough strength to barely lift his head, and he groaned at the tumult of gore and blood that squirmed around his middle - one of the dogs was drawing out another strip of something bloody and ragged - a tattered hawser of tissue that slopped on the floor.

Then suddenly there was no pain, just a spreading numbness that gradually receded until he ceased to see or feel anything, not even the last shred of gut that was teased from him.

He never heard the knock on the door.

CHAPTER TWENTY-THREE

The past year had been so hectic that the silence Alice listened to at night, as she lay awake in her bed, was almost akin to a soothing balm.

Eventually she would fall asleep, drift off into a soundless, cushioned world of long dreams and tarnished memories. It was to this end that Alice began to question whether recent events had made as big an impact on her as she thought - or indeed hoped.

She tried not to think of David but it was a rare day indeed if a tiny scrap of him didn't resurface at some time. Yesterday, she had been relieved when no thought of him had crossed her mind until late in the evening. She refused to nurture it, and slipped it back from whence it came, like a slim volume on a crowded shelf, hoping it would be some time before it was taken down again.

Alice enjoyed lying awake at night, sifting through the scraps of the day, putting things in order and rejecting anything that overwhelmed her thoughts.

She was thinking now of Morag, the woman who rented the apartment downstairs.

Morag was probably older than sixty, a spinster, and carried heavy loneliness around with her like a wet shawl. Once a month, ridiculously early in the morning, Alice would hear Morag jangling her keys, and pulling the front door behind her as she set off to join her rambling club. She attended cake decoration classes mid-week, and made sugar flowers at the weekend. Sometimes in the afternoon, Morag would go into town to catch a matinee performance at the repertory theatre, no doubt ordering a pot of tea and a slice of fruit cake for the interval.

Alice slid her hand across the bed, squares of moonlight swimming on the quilt, and wondered if Morag did this too - aimlessly reaching out for a partner who had yet to exist.

Would she end up like Morag, on her own, scampering around evening classes and symphony halls in her twilight years. What demons would swirl around her, what devils would prod her with their pitchforks? Who was she to say Morag wasn't content? Was she just being arrogant and patronising - assuming that the older woman couldn't possibly be content on her own?

Perhaps she would throw a party soon - a little soiree to provide evidence of her energy, her vitality and tenacity. The girls from the office would come, and perhaps even Morag. It was a small circle of friends when she came to think about it - Morag probably had heaps of close friends.

She would box up his books and the few belongings she still had, and take them round to his flat.

Some of his books had been beyond her. However, no borrowed volume had been as readily devoured as the Lord of the Flies that David lent her, and recommended as his best read ever. She had read that book twice, and remembered wincing when Piggy was killed, when his head opened and stuff came out. The book was so superior to the horror flicks she watched with Maddox - she could watch oozing brains until the cows came home.

There were several CDs that needed sorting - the Mozart

wasn't hers, and neither was Queen's Greatest Hits. Alice was unsure about the Billy Joel - had he wanted it and she'd bought it for him, or was it the other way round - did it matter? She would put it in a box with his other stuff - it was easy enough to make copies these days.

The spare keys to Maddox's apartment lay in her bedside drawer - she only ever used them to let herself in, and had never stayed the night. Alice usually finished her work at the college a good hour or so before he did, and Maddox was rarely at the apartment before her. Where did he go - surely no one could have that many meetings?

Alice would return everything in the morning - take it all back to his apartment to be rid of him for good.

However, her purpose to this end was delayed somewhat by a frantic telephone call the next morning from her mother Jean.

"Alan didn't come home last night!"

Of all the possible thoughts that flitted through her mind at the time - he'd been out drinking, he had been working late, he was having an affair - the one that he might be lying dead in the boot of a car with a Phillips screwdriver stuck through his eye never raised its head.

"He's probably been out on the lash - you know what he's like on a Friday," said Alice.

"But it was shepherd's pie last night, and I'd microwaved some carrots and peas too," said Jean.

"He's probably crashed out somewhere on a sofa."

"You don't think," Jean could hardly believe she was about to say this, "that he's seeing someone else?"

"No Mom - don't be ridiculous, why would you think that? He's been out on the pop - do you want me to come over?"

"No, I'm sure you're right. I'll call you later when he turns up - he'll have to warm up the shepherd's pie but the peas'll be dried to feck."

Alice popped the phone back down on the table, and

wandered into the kitchen. She took a carton of ice cream out of the freezer, and walked over to the window that overlooked the village green. In the cold light of the morning, Alice couldn't face the prospect of going over to Maddox's apartment. Perhaps, she would go round in the afternoon instead. Besides, she had arranged to meet Val for lunch, which would mean at least three courses.

She peeled the lid off the ice cream, and curled up on the window seat with her legs drawn underneath her.

This was a favourite position of hers - face propped up on the heel of a hand, leaning in against the cold glass - it smacked of melancholia and thwarted love. As she dug deep into her raspberry ripple, she imagined how it would appear to the outside world, peering out of this window through a feathered vignette of condensation. However, she was feeling more pragmatic these days - an infinitely preferable state than the love-lorn, bug-eyed rabbit of the past year.

Although it was a Saturday morning, the village green was empty - only Morag could be seen, trotting over to the bus stop.

Morag was carrying a Quality Street tin. Alice was convinced the tin was full of frosted orchids and sugar blossoms.

The Slaughtered Dugong was not Alice's idea of the best place for lunch. It was the nearest pub to the college so consequently she found herself traipsing along her weekday route on her weekend off.

There were many smart and sweet-scented people milling about, elegantly-dressed women and young girls, some with padded shoulders that she was sure had gone out of fashion years ago. Many of the men were suited with glossy white shirts and bright ties. She thought they were probably going on to a wedding.

Val was looking smart in a new leather coat and a pale grey

dress with her hair done up. Alice wasn't sure about the hair, it was pushed back and made her fleshly face look even fuller.

"You look nice with your hair put up like that - and you've lost weight!" said Alice.

Val had already bought the drinks - gin and tonics for both of them, with plenty of ice. Flattened packets of dry roasted peanuts and crisps were splayed around the table. Val licked a finger and began to stab at a few stray crumbs on the table.

"I love people watching," she said. "And you get all sorts in here."

"Yes," said Alice, looking around. "I expect it's always this busy on a Saturday."

"Perhaps we should have gone somewhere quieter?"

"It is fascinating to watch all these people though - I wonder where the wedding is?"

"Probably at the Register Office - I don't see a wedding dress."

"All the friends and relatives are in smart suits."

"Michael Maddox always looks smart in a suit. You both looked stunning on the day," said Val.

Alice checked the rim of her glass for lipstick before taking a slow sip of her drink.

"You don't mind me mentioning it, do you?"

"Of course not. Why should I?" Alice felt as if it was she who had brought up the failed wedding, and not Val. Sensing a shiver of disappointment in her friend, she added: "Although I could never go out with him again - obviously."

"Do you hate him?" asked Val.

"No - I just don't trust him. It would never have worked."

"Some things are just not meant to be," said Val, opening a packet of cheese and onion crisps.

"If truth be told, I was a bit in love with someone else," said Alice.

"Now, if its a man you want, you can, of course, count on me," said Val. "Not straight away but you'd be surprised at how quickly these things can develop. What about Mr Mortimer or Stephen Snodgrass? I think Snoddy is quite taken with you, even if he is a bit of a strange one. You always know what you get with Mr Mortimer, though - there's no mystery there. I saw him in the park the other weekend walking his dogs. Two great hulking brutes they were, but a man who loves his animals is, above all things, a man you can trust. It was a lovely day when I bumped into him - he was throwing sticks."

Always eating, always mooning Val was lecturing her on how to get a man! Her own little admission of being smitten with someone else had fallen on deaf ears.

She took a sip of the gin and tonic, the ice cold against her teeth. There was no need to reiterate her claim - Val was in full flow, and Alice had miscalculated her need to talk about unrequited love. She was pleased that Val had ignored it, and Alice felt quietly satisfied that, after all this time, there was no real measure of catharsis to undergo.

The recognition that his name no longer jumped so readily to her lips, nor caused her insides to pinch suggested David may be on the way to being sluiced out of her life for good. She thought of his lovely gazelle eyes, the large pupils resting under long beaten lashes.

"There's always the Internet," said Val.

"Do people think I need a man?" asked Alice.

"No, but you have to admit you've been out of sorts since the wedding. We're all going to Sandra's flat-warming party next week - why not come along?"

She hadn't been mourning the loss of Maddox - just grieving the impossibility of ever having David. Now that she was over David - over both David and Maddox - she was, and of this she was certain, ready to move on with her life.

Alice would never be able not to respond to those

glittering eyes of David's, but equally she determined never to be held in their thrall.

"I've moved on," said Alice.

Many of the people in the pub had left, wilted carnations and exhausted hair sliding loose as they pushed through the doors. They were all in good spirits, the young and the middle-aged, all good looking and very happy. As she had once been herself, she thought with a trademark sigh.

"What a fantastic colour - that lacey blue dress on that tall girl over there," said Val. "Almost turquoise - it goes so well with those pearls."

"Yes," said Alice. "Let's talk about something else."

CHAPTER TWENTY-FOUR

The exhibition loomed large in Maddox's thoughts, and he wondered about postponing his entry until the following year - putting it off until it was so perfect, no one could ever find fault with it.

He had accessed the website, keyed in both passwords, and was dismayed by the calibre of entrants submitting this year. Although no individual projects had been disclosed, there was enough to suggest the levels of ingenuity were unprecedented.

On the forums, there was even talk of additional categories being created to accommodate some of the more bizarre submissions.

There was also an unsettling rumour that last year's winner - the ever-resourceful Corpuscle - was in the process of creating a piece of work that could even surpass his seminal Archaeopteryx With Glans at the Helsinki Exhibition.

The closing date for submissions was fast approaching, and Maddox was considering an addition to the project.

He wondered if a smaller, more compact version of his work - perhaps laid alongside the main body - would add contrast, or even suggest irrelevance. It was conceivable that such an addition might even have the opposite effect, and detract from the whole.

So many things to think about, too many alternatives to consider, and always, time was tick-tick-ticking away.

Was the project beginning to wane and buckle under the weight of expectation - would he need to seek resolution elsewhere?

From the outset, he had been determined to produce a stand-alone project, which would speak for itself (not literally, of course - although the prospect of producing a working mouth and larynx would have blown all opposition out of the water).

Maddox loosened the straps on the boy's arms and legs, and rubbed at the weals left behind on the smooth skin. Normally he would have pinched the skin to see if there were any signs of life, but in this case it was quite unnecessary.

Both dogs were sated, and lay panting by the sofa, their bellies distended from the feast.

Collecting some dustbin liners from the kitchen, Maddox knew he would need to double, or even triple-bag the rest of the body.

In the kitchen, neatly arranged along the counter, were the pieces he had extracted for the final project - this piece of work that was such a piece of work.

A cool box stood alongside the sink, ready for the stowing.

Maddox mopped up the spills, and scooped up the discarded entrails. The bulbous tubing and twisted knots of gore he dropped in a bucket, which spilled easily into the stout plastic bags.

He then began processing the boy's gutted body.

Leaving the straps in place as a useful leverage, he was in the middle of slicing and hewing when there was a hard knock on the door.

It had taken several hard knocks on the door before Mrs Wardroper answered.

Alice was stood on the step holding a cardboard box taped shut against the elements.

"I was in the back garden," she said. "Those blasted rhododendrons."

"Is Michael in?" asked Alice.

"I don't think so - I saw him leaving earlier in his car."

"Oh," said Alice, instantly regretting the hint of disappointment in her voice. "I'm a colleague of his - you may remember me? I was just returning some of his stuff."

Alice held out the cardboard box.

"Well, you can't leave it here. I can't be doing with things being left in the hallway."

Through the musty hallway, a stray beam of sunlight picked out a puddle of cat basking beneath the open window. It was a dark house - with thick patterned wallpaper showing metallic flowers, and a sturdy staircase running up to a wide landing.

Unlike the terraced properties that lay at the foot of the university campus, the front door of the house wasn't flush against the street, but had a generous swathe of open garden shielded by a thick privet hedge.

"I had a German once, he left two bicycles in the hallway. I can't be doing with bicycles left in the hallway."

Alice knew Maddox's apartment was a couple of flights up to the top floor, and motioned to walk through but Mrs Wardroper barred her way.

"You can't come in - I don't know when he'll be back."

She was a sallow woman, with grass clippings and burrs clinging to her shanks. Her rosy cheeks sat ill with a yellowing complexion, making her appear somewhat outlandish - almost clownish. It was obvious she was protective of her tenants - or had Maddox simply wielded his power and influence over yet another minion?

"I don't want to wait - I'll come back later," said Alice.

197

Maddox answered the front door.

It was the other James - what was he doing here?

Maddox thought that dealing with this particular problem was going to set him back - unless he acted swiftly. He was very picky about killing for the sake of it - all that unnecessary blood, but time was pressing.

He ushered the boy into the house.

Maddox seemed a little flustered, and Jones thought this was unusual, for normally the lecturer was the very epitome of ice and calm.

Jones had spent several hours loitering outside – even returning to the park – before summoning up the courage to knock on the door.

"Yes, he is here," Maddox answered Jones's petulant question. "He's a little tied up at the moment but if you'll come through."

Maddox stepped to one side, and James Jones walked through into the hallway with its turquoise and grey carpet set perfectly in the centre of the floor. The boy didn't notice the carpet - nor did he heed the dead chrysanthemums rattling in the Chinese vase.

The front door was quietly locked behind him.

"I followed you both - from the park," he said.

It was only when he was halfway through the first room that he became aware of the awful cloying smell.

"That'll be young Hawthorn James Smethwick," said Maddox.

James Jones held his nose - he knew well his best friend's propensity to let rip with the most blistering of farts, but this was on a completely different scale altogether.

"I should get some air spray - maybe some Glade," said Maddox.

The room was floored with blonde hardwood, and furnished in plush white leather - darts of vivid red were squirted across it. James Jones never noticed the polished ornaments either, lined up as they were on the mantle, and he hardly glanced at the exquisite chessboard on the small table with the bevelled edges.

Instead, he was looking at his best friend - bled out and folded in two pieces - on a sodden makeshift camp bed.

"It's more portable that way," said Maddox.

James Jones could not take in what he was seeing. Even the yellow rubber gloves, sloshed in red and draped over the sofa seemed to assume a surreal quality. Rubber sheets were rolled up in a corner of the room with saturated sheets of newspaper scrunched up into untidy fat wads. There were bin-liners and rubbish bags scattered around the room, and a couple of fat Alsatians lay snoring by the sofa. On a small table were bottles of chemicals, a flask and a roll of duct tape; also a stainless steel tray of washed saws, sharp chisels and knives, a syringe - some pinking shears.

He looked at his best friend laundered in blood, pressed and folded on a sagging camp bed as if waiting to be posted somewhere. His head was clipped off to one side, and the milky dead eyes were staring at him.

Maddox was studying James Jones's reaction with interest, taking in the rapidly gulping mouth, and the Adam's apple bobbing up and down as if to unleash some unknown hatchling. The wide staring eyes, the colour a strange liquid blue he hadn't noticed before. The boy's blanched complexion pulled itself down through the collar of his shirt, and his hands clasped and unclasped as though seeking purchase on the foul air itself. He probably would need a selection of scented candles and deodorising sprays now that he came to think about it. James Jones's hands really were podgy - he would kill for the porcelain smoothness of Jonathan Mortimer's hands.

There was a slight wavering catch to the boy's voice - a tremulous gurgle almost.

"What the f..."

"It's what I do."

Maddox was reluctant to begin another harvesting. Although raw materials were always of use to him, it would be too time consuming at this stage to prepare sufficiently. The preliminary work itself took up huge chunks of time - all the scrubbing and shaving and clipping back - the securing with tape and straps and harness - the binding and the butchery.

It was the tiniest clink behind him that caused Jones to turn around. Maddox had unclipped a Persian ceremonial dagger from its mounting on the wall. It was an exquisite blade - sharp with brass mounts on the leather scabbard, and cross-form brass hilts along the handle.

"Please – no," James Jones croaked.

"Yes," Maddox said.

"No," he repeated.

"Yes."

"Oh, God, no."

"Oh, God, yes," Maddox said.

It was late in the evening when both of the James's were eventually cleaned up and packed away.

Maddox was dissatisfied with the second killing - it wasn't remorse, but any necessary harvesting had to be targeted and pursued for its own singular beauty. The result had to rest on more than aesthetic merit - it was the state of the art that mattered - an essential precision that provided the impetus behind the whole exacting business.

Maddox put the bodies into the plastic bags, securely doubling-up, and tying them tightly with twisty wire ties. The room needed meticulous cleaning from top to bottom, and he carefully scoured the furniture and floor for any tissue that might have gone awry.

The dogs were bloated. Maddox herded them back into their pens where he put down plenty of dog biscuits and water to last the couple of days until Mortimer returned. They could do with losing a bit of weight now anyway.

After piling the slopping wet bags into the lined boot of his car, Maddox drove the short distance back to his apartment where his landlady lay in wait.

"A young lady called round to see you," said Mrs Wardroper.

"A young lady?"

"She wanted to leave some stuff, but I couldn't be doing with it," Mrs Wardroper folded her arms. "Not after that business with the German and his bicycles."

The duodenum slid smoothly between his long, bony fingers as he held it up to the light, admiring the fine translucent quality of the tissue. Deflated strips of intestine were massaged into ribbed lengths of cord – they glistened and twanged as he pulled them gently apart. The liver was smooth and weighty - he slid his hand across the cool surface, cupping its satisfying bounty in both hands.

Then it was the turn of Hawthorn James's kidneys to be appraised – irresistible and blood-brown, smooth as river-washed pebbles.

He gently padded the kidneys down in small dishes, and placed them carefully in the freezer beneath the crinkle-cut chips and ice cream. Drawing each tissue and organ out of the cool box, Maddox could hardly contain his glee, and he almost cried out when he beheld the most delightful pancreas he had seen for a long time. Surely now, the prize was within his reach.

Who would have thought that within that scrawny, oddly elongated torso of young Hawthorn James Smethwick there would be all these glorious gewgaws? He mentally ticked off each of his acquisitions, confirming that he did indeed need only a simple pair of eyes and some nice, thick hair to finally complete the project.

Soon he would begin the final construction - it would not take long now that all the pieces were finally falling into place.

Boyd and Hettie lived out in the countryside, and from the narrow approach road of their smallholding, Maddox could see Hettie as she bustled past the corrugated sheds. She was wearing a long skirt with white daisies stitched along the hem. Fountains of gnats danced around her head, and it seemed as if she hadn't changed her clothes since the last time he had seen her. The collar and cuffs were similarly embroidered, the whole ensemble topped off with a pair of green Wellington boots. Around her shoulders, she was wearing the same cardigan that she always did.

"More nosh for the boys," Maddox said, pulling a couple of weighty black bin liners from the back of his car. "Lead me to the grinder."

The door to the utility room was already open, and Maddox could see that a fresh batch of minced meat and bone meal had already been prepared for the ferrets. Next to the grinder there was a couple of mugs of steaming coffee, and a plate of chocolate Hobnobs.

Boyd appeared in the doorway with a bucket of water and a scrubbing brush – nodding, he rarely ever spoke.

"Tea or coffee?" said Hettie.

"No thanks," said Maddox. "I'm in a bit of a rush actually."

"You can leave the meat there, if you like - I can grind it up later."

"No, it's OK - I can do it."

It didn't take long - it was mainly guts and entrails and, curiously, a snippet of intestine containing an appendix. He snipped it off and wrapped it carefully in a tissue - it might come in useful for the final submission.

Hettie sipped her coffee and nibbled on a Hobnob, brushing off crumbs, and breaking off a piece to feed to one of the ferrets.

It was a pretty little animal, Maddox thought, with a dark mask banding its eyes. He offered it a tiny bloody scrap of

Hawthorn James, which it snapped up with relish. Emptying the rest of the meat into the grinder, Maddox then poured some bone meal into the bowl to help absorb the blood better.

Then he helped himself to a Hobnob.

CHAPTER TWENTY-FIVE

"I expect," said Val, "if they put Dancing Queen on, everyone will get up and dance."

"I hope they don't," said Jackie. "I hate ABBA."

Only two people were dancing - it was nearly nine thirty, and Alice knew the party wouldn't be in full swing for another couple of hours. Several colleagues had turned up, having made their way from the Slaughtered Dugong. Sandra said Maddox and Snodgrass might come along later as well.

Grumpy Frank took a swig from his can, mumbling that he didn't trust Maddox - wouldn't give you the steam, he said.

Val was wearing her hair up, and had arrived at the party in a once-loose blue dress - Alice had plumped for her sparkly white mica top yet again, with the favourite black skirt. Jackie, her hair rigid and unmoving, was carrying off a retro look with a cashmere tie-neck cardigan.

"There's not much of a buffet," said Val, eyeing a celery dip with barely concealed contempt. "We could order a few pizzas - I'm sure Sandra wouldn't mind."

Sandra was minding Ross at the far end of the room,

pressed into him with a voracious tongue exploring his mouth.

"She'll have to come up for air at some time," said Val.

Through a tangle of people in the doorway, Maddox strode into the room, appearing to fill every space and beyond - an undeniable presence - people were left in his wake. His appearance caused Sandra to break away from Ross, and gallop over to him, her arms waving wildly.

"You're here!" she squealed, standing on tip toes to kiss him, and even Alice found it difficult to dismiss the charisma of the man.

"I did say I would try to come," he said. "But I'm afraid I can't stay long."

Sandra wrapped her arms around him - a little too snuggly, Alice thought - as Maddox smiled and scanned the room. It was a large flat - two of the walls scraped clear of wallpaper, with tentative swatches of emulsion brushed over drying plaster. Although the evenings were getting lighter, there was a murkiness outside where ancient, bricked terraces glowered across narrow streets. The room seemed gloomy despite the twinkling fairy lights and orange lamps that Sandra deemed appropriate to the occasion.

A generic buffet of crisps, cocktail sausages, pastries and peanuts were strewn upon a long trestle table - a bowl of fruit punch stood on a counter, its ladle dripping tight splashes on the floor. A scattering of flat-warming presents and cards lay heaped in a corner of the room - the ubiquitous potted plants and chopping boards, a fluffy toy with a spotted bow-tie.

"To celebrate your new home - I hope you'll be very happy here," he said, handing Sandra a wrapped gift.

Sandra squealed but didn't say anything more.

Maybe she wouldn't throw a party herself after all, Alice thought - they were such dull affairs if you didn't get the right mix. She didn't really know the right people - how can you tell who the right people are anyway? Perhaps she should ask Morag? Even David, her ultimate perfect person had turned out to be an awkward square peg in a round hole.

Maddox walked over to Alice.

Bold as brass, thought Alice, who was never one to let a good cliché go to waste.

"Hello, Alice."

"Hello, Michael."

He acknowledged Val and Jackie with the faintest of bows, a mannerism not even faintly ridiculous coming from this most effortless of men. Maddox smiled, the eye-tooth seemed even whiter and deadlier.

"How are you?" asked Alice, immediately regretting being the first to ask.

"I'm very well, thanks."

Maddox was slowly watching the room, like a predator on the savannah.

"And you?"

"Fine, good - couldn't be better."

More people were arriving - Snodgrass and Mortimer came scurrying across to join them. Snodgrass had brought along a bottle of sweet sherry.

"It wasn't cheap," he said, placing the sherry on the table with the other bottles.

Snodgrass began talking to Maddox, his excitable Adam's apple thrumming up and down. Mortimer picked at the bowl of peanuts, taking one at a time instead of a handful.

"We should have stayed at the Dugong a bit longer, it hasn't really got going yet," said Val.

"I might go soon anyway," said Alice. "I'm not really in the mood."

Maddox suddenly appeared at her side with a gin and tonic.

"Plenty of ice," he said.

She took the drink, unsure what to say, and desperately hoped she didn't look in any way uncomfortable.

"The way you like it," he added.

"Thank you."

Alice was uneasy, unsure whether to demur or protest - she had a right to protest, damn it, and Maddox seemed to fully realise this.

Val nudged Jackie with her elbow, affecting a nonchalance neither of them felt, nor cared for.

"These olives are horrible," said Val, eating five in one go. "I wonder where the pizzas have got to?"

Slowly they moved further down the table, picking at the nibbles.

"Alice, I really can't explain, nor justify what I did that day - I can only hope you'll forgive me."

"It was no big deal - not for me anyway."

"Of course it was a big deal, but I assure you - I never, ever had any intention of hurting you in any way."

"I guess when you left me at that altar, you didn't think that maybe I'd be a little bit miffed - a little bit put out?"

A hot coal of anger had suddenly been stoked and left smouldering on the grate.

Snodgrass and Mortimer inched along the table, suddenly keen to appraise the sausage rolls.

"Of course not - I realise how devastated you must have been."

"Big of you."

"You're right, I'm sorry - I had no right to bring it up again."

"I must go."

Alice looked around for a non-existent coat, before taking leave of Sandra who took her tongue out of Ross's mouth, and begged her to reconsider.

"But you've only just got here."

"I'm sorry, San - I've a bit of a headache - it's been coming on all day."

"Umm...but...peh, peh, peh...stay...sleh," said Sandra, trying to speak and nuzzle the tip of Ross's tongue at the same time.

After Alice left, Maddox finished his drink and placed the glass on the table. He held a light jacket in the crook of his arm, and nodded briefly to Val and Jackie as if tipping his hat.

"I must go myself," he said.

CHAPTER TWENTY-SIX

A few drops of rain speckled the windscreen, and Inspector Lively scowled at the greasy, grey clouds - he couldn't imagine a grimier start to the day.

He opened the car door, and tipped the remains of the coffee from his flask on to the ground. From the car park on the edge of the woods, he could see straight through the trees and across the wide meadow. Yesterday, he chased off some kids who were throwing stones at the ornamental fountain by the playground. The local vandals were always knocking off the cedar shingles on the fountain roof, and Archie lately found himself becoming increasingly in favour of enforced sterilisation.

He unwrapped the silver foil from a sausage roll and took a couple of huge bites, working the pastry into his mouth as he adjusted the rear-view mirror. He wouldn't want anyone to think he was shirking - surveillance was a duty he took seriously, and the local yobs had been an ongoing problem.

With retirement in the offing, there had been long, complex issues around his recent duties. When Archie first joined the force, his inspector had adopted a head in the sand solution to any problems, throwing most of his manpower into meeting quotas on other crime. Burglaries and neighbourhood disputes fell to Archie, and he did a decent enough job with his plodding, methodical prowess. It was the same now - except he was the inspector, but rather than quotas and targets, his concern lay more in smoothing over operations, holding tides at bay until he could sail off into his own personal sunset.

He pulled the blanket across his knees - it was a bit chilly. Soon he would meet up with PC Walduck at the Pavilion, the refurbished cafe by the adjoining golf course. A quick brew, and a cheeky bacon sarnie with brown sauce would shore him up for the rest of the morning.

Then he really must talk to the parents of the missing boys. Some people called it procrastination - he called it a complete pain in the ass. He noted the vernacular - many US police shows had made their mark on him over the years. Tolkien College seemed to be at the heart of the recent missing persons scenarios. With the hippy teacher going missing in the Lake District, and now these lads, it was becoming something of a Bermuda Triangle for the unfixed. In fact, if you included the landscape gardener who still hadn't turned up, there was something of a local missing theme running through all the disappearances. Even the husband of a couple they had interviewed had gone missing. He was sure there must be a connection - several people had been interviewed already but there wasn't much to go on.

PC Walduck came on air to announce his arrival at the Pavilion. He was getting a brew in, and the bacon was on the sizzler.

It was quiet this time of the morning - his unmarked vehicle rarely got much attention, the area warden actively welcoming an intermittent police presence. Encouraging emails would be sent to the Chief Constable regarding the sterling surveillance work Inspector Lively was undertaking

- especially with regards to keeping the vandalism under control. Railing fences had already been put up at great cost along the perimeter so joy-riding and fly-tipping was no longer an issue. Archie still liked to keep an eye on things though, especially keen to rebuke any dog-walkers who allowed their pets to crap along the paths.

The two lads had only recently been reported as missing but it was impossible to pinpoint the exact day of their disappearance, as both sets of parents had been absent from home at the time. Archie could feel a 'tsk' coming on. His wife hadn't wanted children any more than he did but surely they'd do a better job of raising a family than some people.

Still, he had a few more dollar days to get through before his retirement.

At this time of morning, the Pavilion was busy with several of his colleagues tucking into fry-ups and grills - there was no muesli in sight. They had either finished their shifts, or were half-way through them.

He greeted them all, exchanging some winning banter with PC Walduck, and shaking hands with Inspector Brownlow. Archie hadn't seen Brownlow for a while, but knew him well from the early days when they worked together - not with the police force but in the prison service.

"Not long now, Archie," said Brownlow. "You'll soon have more time on your hands than you'll know what to do with it."

"I won't be bored - you can be sure of that."

"I've already got my name down for an allotment."

"Trust me - you don't want to go there."

Somewhat systematic of his internal career compass, Archie once investigated a dispute at the local allotment. He expected vegetable abuse or a smashed cold frame or two. He certainly wasn't prepared for the contempt held by some tenants against their fellow gardeners. Particular scorn was reserved for anyone trespassing on individual plots as rivalries and warring factions broke out across the fruit and veg - several greenhouses were burned down, water tanks poisoned and prize marrows disemboweled.

"There was a retired rear admiral at the allotment," said Archie, "who was Master Gardener for two years, and had hopes of taking a third title until someone stamped on his hollyhocks."

Brownlow said that there were so many plans for his retirement, a spreadsheet would be needed to contain them. He was a pug of a man, features pushed deep within his face like buttons in dough, yet his eyes still held the ice-blue clarity of his youth - blue chinks in a set face. Somewhat at odds with this, he was graced with a delicate and fastidious manner - traits which confused colleagues and baffled his prison charges.

Archie thought back to his time as a warder at the city prison. He had started his first day being escorted to the cell block through an outdoor yard. The gloomy Gothic bulk of the building loomed large around him with hundreds of murky glass columns in the walls, densely packed like cobbles on a street. These were the windows to the cells, and Archie had couched out a thin smile when he heard a bunch of large keys jangling somewhere behind him.

He eagerly assumed any mantle of seniority that could be thrown his way, but never quite forged ahead in his career. This was before he decided on joining the police force - before he wondered if there was a more interesting career path to wend his way down - an easier one, perhaps?

Glancing down at PC Walduck's newspaper, the spread pages liberally splotched with brown sauce, Archie read that Aston Villa had conceded yet again in the last minute of a game.

"Bunch of wasters," he grumbled.

At the prison, it was the noise that troubled him most. He could hear it from the locker room where he had been assigned locker number sixty-six. He could remember standing up straight, pulling his shoulders together - the prescribed mechanics of a callow youth on his first day. A terrible uproar of bleating and yelling, echoing whistles and laughter, squabbling arguments, bellows and cracked sobbing. The air stagnant in the corridors - a mixture of misery and resignation, coated with an underlying fug of numbed men. It seemed some prisoners were celebrities - kept apart from the other inmates in special wings. He recalled the prison being criticised at the time by its own Board of Visitors for being too soft on prisoners.

"I'm glad I got out of the prison service," said Brownlow, pulling a particularly resistant rind from a rasher. "What with all these changes taking place."

It was rumoured that thousands of prisoners could lose their automatic access to gym equipment, games consoles and other perks under plans for a tough new regime in Britain's jails. The Justice Secretary was busy finalising urgent proposals to combat right-wing complaints suggesting that prisons were too lax.

Under the plan, it would become harder for prisoners to earn the right to perks. Ministers were planning on increasing the threshold of good behaviour, requiring prisoners to work or enrol in education courses in order to receive privileges. Sky television would be banned in private prisons and discussions were under way into whether it was practical to make thousands of inmates wear prison uniform rather than their own clothes.

The moves were likely to alarm prison governors at a time of overcrowding and budget cuts, leading to inmates being locked in their cells for longer, increasing tension among prisoners and making the job of running them more difficult.

For some reason, Archie found himself thinking of Michael Maddox - it was strange that he should do so now. It faintly troubled him that his steadfast refusal to delve too

213

deeply into Maddox's past was beyond his capacity for reproach.

"I've never been keen on interesting times," said Archie.

He walked to the huge windows of the Pavilion and pulled aside a plastic blind. It was still raining, as it always seemed to do these days - a light, determined drizzle falling on the lush slopes of the golf course and the woods beyond. A solitary golfer was stoically swinging away amid the divots, and three magpies desultorily pecked around the picnic benches for discarded rinds and shrunken fruit.

PC Walduck appeared at his side, a lick of sauce clinging to his bottom lip.

"I'm all charged up and ready to roll," he said.

"Best be off, then," said Archie. "Sooner we finish talking with the parents, the quicker we can get to the pub."

CHAPTER TWENTY-SEVEN

Stephen Snodgrass stood in front of the creative writing class, which was strangely subdued without the two James's. He didn't know where they had got to but he hoped something bad had happened to them.

He glanced at his wristwatch.

She was late.

The eminent poet Jarinder Shinybeetle had a fierce reputation, having only agreed to visit the school and recite poetry if allowed to swear. Apparently it was essential to the delivery and potency of her verse. In her deep fruity voice, she said questions would be welcome about the intensity of her rhythms and imagery, but insisted no references be made to her lesbian live-in lover, Penelope Briskett. Despite being reassured that it was a creative writing class she was addressing, and not an awards presentation, Ms Shinybeetle was adamant on two types of mineral water being made available, and a packet of Opal Fruits.

"They are not Starburst - they are Opal Fruits. Starburst implies a celestial flavour which is a ridiculous assumption for a sweet."

"Opal Fruits it is then," said Snodgrass.

Snodgrass had accrued some serious kudos for inviting the radical poet in the first place. As a result, the creative writing class was surprisingly well attended, and he was genuinely relieved that the two James's hadn't bothered to turn up. It wasn't often that the department hosted guest speakers, and Ms Shinybeetle was very topical at the moment after her infamous stint on the South Bank Show when she had trotted out an inglorious tribute to the Duke and Duchess of Cambridge.

He had hoped to use some of her loose, impenetrable prose as a good example of writing which universally opposed the conventions of the English language. But now, with time ticking away, he was thinking more and more about the Pot Noodle he had waiting for him in the staff room.

As unofficially mooted by the Tolkien College marking policy, he would eventually pass most of the class, dish out a couple of Merits and the odd Distinction, and refer as few students as possible for the following academic year.

The students were mulling over Ms Shinybeetle's latest anthology, hastily formulating their questions for the forthcoming session. He ran a finger down the class timetable, and saw that the reading week was imminent.

Students were invited to use this week to catch up on assignments and research. For the Department of English Language and Literature, it presented a chunk of free time to explore new slants on existing modules or, as in this case, enjoy a good old fashioned jolly in the Lake District at the college's expense.

He had just spent a few days there with Mortimer, and was eager to get back. It would present an ideal opportunity for Snodgrass to flex his outdoor muscles - to impress his new colleagues. However, he had reckoned without Maddox.

Bridling even now, he recalled the dismissive manner in which Maddox downed his proposed itinerary at the previous meeting. It told him something about the nature of the man. Snodgrass's mouth had hinged open, like a panting grouper, as he watched Maddox strike out and delete all of his suggestions. He was convinced Maddox hadn't gone within spitting distance of a Gore-Tex jacket in his life.

Maddox was keen to keep all activities local rather than go traipsing over the fells and hills. He had little interest in rock climbing - suggesting it should be optional - and favoured archery and less demanding pursuits instead.

Mortimer spanieled around Maddox, consenting to every suggestion and alteration put forward. It had been no contest at all - Maddox easily overwhelmed him, winning favour on every decision.

How Mortimer had fluttered around Maddox - a moth-dog with lolling tongue and ridiculous big brown eyes.

An unnerving thought suddenly struck him - how would he feel if Maddox bested him on the rugged rock faces and plummeting drops? It wasn't as if that was unlikely either - the man possessed muscle to his lean frame - sharp and wolfish with a languid reach to his limbs that spoke of untapped resources.

He irritably looked at his watch - it was a quarter past two.

Ms Shinybeetle appeared to have a diva-like penchant for scorning the accepted rituals of timetables and appointments.

And her poetry was shit too.

CHAPTER TWENTY-EIGHT

The eyes glaze over after death.

It was a feature that always disappointed Maddox. Those lovely copper brown eyes had been reduced to dead fish eyes on a monger's slab, the degradation of colour faded to an opaque sheen like an unripe fruit peeled of its husk.

Maddox lifted more baskets out of the freezer, and placed the little dishes of tissues and organs on a table. He lifted out a skull and held it up to the light.

Not quite a fellow of infinite jest, he thought - and certainly not abhorred in my imagination.

He smiled and lowered the skull, nudging a small folded blanket under the head to prop it a little. Straightening up, he held the small of his back, and stretched before returning to work. The hair was the real problem - dark brown tresses had been intricately woven with thick strands of grey-flecked black hair and, despite creating a softer, gentler surround, it still suggested a degree of compromise.

It was not starkly evident but even such minor imperfections may prove crucial in the final reckoning.

In the wardrobe there was more hair, garnered and stored

in a selection of boxes and parcels. Hat boxes were ideal containers and, in a way, quite appropriate. Browsing the various samples of hair had proved unsatisfactory, no swatches deemed suitable for the final submission, each style lacking the fine lustrous bulk he was striving for - that halo of vibrancy in which to set his stone. He would be leaving soon for the Lake District - for the team-building exercise - having first promised an appreciative Jonathan Mortimer that he would pick him up on the way.

However, he still had a few things to do before setting off.

Picking up his mug of coffee, he walked over to the desk in the alcove, and switched on the lamp. Pulling back the blinds, he then popped open his laptop, and logged onto the website. Staring at the page that rode up in front of him, his eyes narrowed, and the long canine bared itself in what was almost a low growl.

Corpuscle was the favourite to achieve a successive victory for his work - even though there was no indication to what form his submission might take.

He scrolled further down the page, and saw his own pseudonym highlighted as 'one to watch,' which did little to assuage the white-hot rage within him. He began to seethe - was he the only one to regard Corpuscle's recent work as derivative and scratchy - just a little repetitive? The creative output was not at issue here - Corpuscle was a prodigious artist whose back catalogue alone would take steely resolve and years of dedication to surpass.

Surely now was the time for change - the arena ripe for a new direction. And who could doubt that he, Michael Maddox - the one to watch - would elevate the exhibition to new unprecedented levels of genius.

There was little time to re-assess the project, but the team-building session in the Lake District may provide some last minute opportunities to embellish it.

From a drawer under his desk, he pulled out a thin stamped letter of confirmation, and held it under the light.

A refrigerated van had already been hired for the long journey to the Ukrainian border, and would be ready for collection on his immediate return from the Lake District. All the documents were valid and in good order, the necessary passwords noted and memorised - the contacts for transit and disposal alerted.

An arranged rendezvous in Krakow with the agency was also firmly in place - detailed maps of the Carpathian Mountains had been mailed to him with coded directions to an ancient forest. Final arrangements would be dispatched to him before the end of the week. A key and combination number would also be sent to him separately for the gallery, its exact location withheld until the final preparations were in place.

It had been so much easier last year when the exhibition was held in Ashby-de-la-Zouch.

Maddox scrolled through the pages, checking various forums and blogs, but he could see little to unsettle him further, and quickly signed out.

He had just enough time to check out a few websites before setting out. He searched for coloured contact lenses - it would be a shame if he couldn't resurrect the lustre of those poor dead eyes.

Then he really must get going - Jonathan Mortimer would be waiting anxiously for him, wringing those perfect little hands of his.

Alice was sure the Billy Joel CD was hers after all, and could see no point in letting Maddox have it. She had brought a box of his stuff into college, determined to drop it back at Maddox's flat while he was away in the Lakes - never mind the fusty old landlady, she would use the spare keys and be damned.

As she rummaged in her desk for some scissors and tape, her hand fell upon a photograph she hadn't seen for some time. It was a picture of David and Simon from the previous summer - a photograph swiped from her brother's room ages ago. It showed David with bare torso, tanned and healthy, grinning giddily at the camera. There were alarmingly large tufts of tawny hair spouting from his armpits, and the smooth lines of his surprisingly curvy body were wrapped at waist-level by a huge white towel. He was, for some absurd reason, sporting yellow and green wristbands. His flashing smile and beautiful eyes beamed out of the photograph at her.

There were also several college photographs saved in a file on her computer, involving alumni-related events and open days. Part of her brief was to produce a twice-yearly newsletter, which was mailed out to all the ex-students, former staff and governors of the college so any relevant articles naturally ended up on her desk. Some of these featured the enigmatic Mr Maddox, and she idly tapped one of them open.

It was a good photograph - a three-quarter shot. Maddox was clearly a very photogenic man - his teeth shone as he addressed a group of students during a college open day. It was a shame that the flash had reflected so violently off that smile for the characteristic eye-tooth had been swallowed up in the glare. But nothing could blur those eyes of his. There was a dark rim to his irises that Alice couldn't remember noticing before, as if someone in an editing suite - an artist or colourist - had edged a dry brush around the eyes. There were other photographs, which showed his face in profile, or underexposed, but always looking somewhat calculating and predatory. In one of the later photographs, Maddox's generous brows pitched tight shadows just above the lids, making the eyes shine with a brilliant emerald intensity that could almost be described as deadly.

Alice switched her attention back to David's own glorious eyes, and tried to deflect the memory back into a less accessible corner of her mind. It was seldom these days that those unsinkable fragments of him floated across her thoughts, and when they did, they would pitch and toss irritably until she dealt with them.

It had been quite a while since she had last seen David, even though she was completely over him (nothing from Inner Voice?) Simon hadn't seen David for nearly a week now, and she wondered if they had fallen out. Ridiculously, she hoped they had.

The late afternoon sun was raising swirling mirages on the college quadrant, and the plants on the window shone with an elastic luminosity. Alice fumbled in her handbag for the compact. Flicking it open, she smoothed the faint lines around her eyes and mouth - smudging them down but not out of sight. Her eyes looked tired - they were still nothing remotely like anthracite.

Her coat was back in the staff room, so she switched off her computer, needlessly shuffled some paper on her desk, and pushed her chair back.

"Well, that's me done."

"Are you going to the Dugong?" asked Val, breaking off several panels of Garibaldi in one go.

"I think I'll give it a miss. There're a few things I want to get done tonight."

"Not even a quick one?"

"No - I think I'll head off."

She locked her desk - the long brass keys to Maddox's apartment dangled from the key-ring.

It was best to get these things over and done with.

Alice wasn't a fan of procrastination but perhaps a quick one at the Dugong wouldn't hurt. Maddox would be in the Lake District for a while yet - there was plenty of time to return his stuff, and she could definitely use a drink.

Alice waved over to Val.

Snodgrass had secured a quote and provisional booking for a corporate package at an old quarry customised for outdoor pursuits. The quarry, deep on the west side of the forest, was screened by thick woodland, and swathes of tall ferns and bracken.

They were gathered in the lounge, settled on the orange sofas and purple cushions. It was generally agreed that Snodgrass would lead the morning archery session, and organize orienteering and rock climbing for later in the day.

"I suggest everyone should come with me in the afternoon," Snodgrass proposed. "After the archery."

"I'm not keen," said Jonathan Mortimer.

"If the quarry is free all day, those who want to continue archery may do so," said Maddox.

"We can go rock climbing, and do some fell walking," Snodgrass enthused.

"I don't like rocks," said Mortimer.

"Rock climbing is not compulsory," said Maddox.

Snodgrass's face darkened.

The lounge door clicked open, and Maddox's face brightened when the tantalising coiffure of Jackie came into view. Jackie was one of the few additional recruits signed up when Principal Richardson insisted the team-building event should be open to all staff. Jackie had recently washed her hair but rather than pile it up in her usual austere style, she had let it loose and it flowed about her shoulders. The liberating effect of the freed hair evoked a sense of frizzed tar let loose.

The result was quite staggering to say the least - this really could be the final piece to the project - it was just the black he was looking for - thick and inky. Maddox had always considered the eyes as the focal point of his piece, but it was the hair he needed most of all now - he really could not leave without it.

How come he had never noticed Jackie's hair before? He was slightly concerned about the logistics of adding to the project if additional material needed be conveyed from such a remote area. But with what he had in mind, the remoter the better.

All great artists are never satisfied with their final output, and ceaselessly strive to improve upon their work. Maddox was no exception to this discipline. There was another point, to which he was also a keen subscriber - that a truly great artist must know when to let go, when to concede there is nothing left to give. Now that he had the eyes, the finishing touch to his masterpiece would be the hair.

It would be his crowning glory.

CHAPTER TWENTY-NINE

Stephen Snodgrass was quietly sipping on a carton of cranberry fruit juice when the crossbow bolt went searing through the air and straight into his throat, pinning him against a tree.

"Bugger!" Maddox cursed and lowered the crossbow. The one piece of Snodgrass that he may have used was now splattered against some mulchy old tree bark. The man's extraordinary bobbing Adam's apple would be of no use now - it might have been a nice little bolt of gristle to sew under the skin.

Maddox had trained himself to think of the aiming and firing as one single action but his shot sequence was off. He was hoping for a nice tidy chest shot, or perhaps the inverted notch beneath the sternum. Despite clicking off the safety, and keeping the cross-hairs steady on Snodgrass's chest, he obviously jerked too hard on the final shot.

The early morning session had not augured well. During the initial practice in the quarry, Maddox's long fingers had loosed the first fletch over the targets, and into a patch of scrub beyond - much to the glee of Snodgrass. The instructor from the centre was patient and encouraging, but it still took a little longer before Maddox could find the target. Even Jackie seemed to have better technique than he did, and freed a couple of arrows unerringly into their marks.

Snodgrass had finally managed to work more abseiling and rock climbing into the schedule, and was due to supervise some dizzy traverses while Maddox oversaw the archery. However, the chance to showcase his talent, after consistently hitting the inner rings during the morning session - whereas Maddox's own efforts rarely troubled the target - was too good an opportunity to miss.

He had enjoyed this rare show of superiority, and even offered a few pointers regarding draw strength and stance.

The condescension was not lost on Maddox.

With Snodgrass keen to cement his marksmanship, the afternoon schedule was put on hold, and the remaining staff needed no further invitation to head to the pub.

Only a few remained - an unfortunate few.

Maddox nocked another bolt to the crossbow, and looked around him, peering intently through the swathes of foliage that encircled the quarry, but there was no one left.

The forest was deathly quiet.

He let the weapon slip from his hand into a patch of springy bracken, and then strode over to release Snodgrass from his pinioned position. He was still gurgling a little but the eyes were already beginning to powder over into that familiar glaucous sheen that he had become accustomed to.

The bracken was wonderfully high, a fountain of bright green and tawny browns, the perfect cover for his bags and wrappings. Not that he needed much for the meagre selection he had collected so far - it had all been very disappointing with only a few real prizes.

From a plastic liner bag, chilled with ice, he pulled out one of Mortimer's hands. It was a beautiful, deft little thing with only the ragged stump marring the overall effect. Not so much of the elbow was needed but there was still further use for the fingers.

Wiping the shaft of the crossbow with a cloth, Maddox then proceeded to curl Mortimer's fingers around the weapon, pulling the thumbs across the bowstring, and pushing the fleshy pads of the fingers deep in against the wood. He wasn't sure how much of a fingerprint would be left by a dead mans fingers but surely the whorls and spirals wouldn't have sunk too far back into the skin.

His own long and bony fingers easily straddled the dainty hands of the former Director of English Language and Literature. Was there any point to this, he wondered - would the inevitable forensic examination rumble a trail so falsely and ineptly laid - would there be tearful laughter at his futile efforts? It was no matter really - a mere delaying tactic if anything.

In the aftermath of the killings, no one would ever really question whether Mortimer was responsible for slaying Snodgrass.

If the hands could have been taken without harming Mortimer, he would have done so. However, such reasoning was unrealistic, and not in keeping with the clinical execution of his work. At least he owed Mortimer that much - he was now undeniably part of the project.

The exhibition would be a less weather-beaten epitaph to the man than a dreary tombstone - no lichen would unseemly encroach upon such a memorial.

It was amazing how long Mortimer had lived with both arms lopped off.

The spurting had been astonishing, but eventually he had dropped to his knees, mouth gaping and, for once, the severed cloth of his shirt anything but stiff, white and starchy. Those puppy dog eyes were still blinking up at him as he keeled over into the bracken while Maddox wiped the blood from the machete.

He had popped the arms in a zip-lock bag, tucking them into the iced plastic liner, and storing them in the root hollow of a beech.

Poor old Jonathan Mortimer - he had been quite fond of the man but his contribution now would be of much more significant value.

The tiny frisson of excitement Mortimer felt as Maddox stole up behind him to compliment his open stance evaporated with the first slash from the machete. He rolled the corpse over into a shallow ditch, the abbreviated stumps waving lustily with their clotted gore.

The body was not alone.

The disappointment of finding out Jackie's hair was anything but natural - the woven hairpiece had come undone in his hands - jarred him. He would have to forego the hair now, and make do with what he had - there simply wasn't enough time. Looking around the clearing for Jackie's head, he was relieved to see it had fetched up in the bole of an ancient oak.

There was also a fine pair of ear lobes from the instructor, which may be worth attaching to the final piece.

Mortimer's body would probably begin to smell soon unless his erstwhile pristine manager deferred such malodorous practices even in death. He gathered up some woody stems of gorse, and pulled several large ferns into place, tenting the shallow graves with bracken. It was going to be a busy old evening paddling these last few out onto the lake.

Maddox was expecting to be on foreign soil soon, revelling in the great hall of the exhibition - to be crowned as the worthy successor to Corpuscle.

The reverberations from his submission would ripple out - the repercussions felt for years to come. The culmination of his work was almost upon him - and the confidence, which the resulting enterprise instilled in him, was impossible to unseat.

Only recently, the newspapers had published photographs of the missing two James's. It was a pity about the unflattering photograph of James Jones - his mother would have enough to contend with if she ever found out what had happened to him, without a bulbous, jowly shot of her son peering out from the front page.

He would have a final clear up, a last sortie across the lake, and then head back.

He needed to be on his way.

CHAPTER THIRTY

Alice couldn't believe she had left it so late to go to Maddox's apartment - he was due back any day soon, and she still hadn't dropped his stuff off. Procrastination was a trait she deplored in others - it was a simple task, and little more. She would return Maddox's possessions, minus the Billy Joel CD - and get the hell out of there.

Arms clutched around the cardboard box, she looked up at the large Victorian house. The vestibule door had been closed shut, and the front door pulled to.

She was surprised to find her hands shaking, her mouth dry - feeling a little anxious and gulpy.

Alice was sure it was the photograph that did it - she had been thinking of David again - that gorgeous smile and those beguiling eyes. Here she was at Maddox's front door and thinking about David - keys clutched in her hot hand.

Simon still hadn't seen him for a while, and Alice felt a sting of panic barb through her - what if she never saw those glorious eyes again?

Stepping up to the door, she turned the first key, clicking it open, and pushed through into the hall with its floral swirls and speckled sunbeams. There was no sign of the landlady, the house seeming deathly quiet and becalmed. A tortoiseshell cat looked in through the low windows and mewled.

The old house creaked and squeaked as Alice made her way up to Maddox's apartment on the top floor, dust motes dancing in the low light. She lightly knocked on the door as she turned the key, walking defiantly through into the empty apartment.

In the small kitchen, she poured herself a glass of water, and grimaced - the water was tepid, unpleasantly warm to her taste.

It needed ice - she needed ice.

Maddox pulled onto the gravelled forecourt of the house, a spray of grit shot out from underneath the wheels and zinged the tortoiseshell cat. The animal yowled and fled under the hydrangeas. Maddox couldn't believe how quickly it had taken him to drive back from the Lake District - the roads had been so quiet, and now there was nothing to stop him leaving for the exhibition.

He just had to collect the exhibit.

There had been no point completing his stay in the Lake District - he had harvested all he needed and disposed of the rest. He would have liked to visit Boyd and Hettie for one last grind, but time was of essence. Maddox had called ahead and arranged to pick up the refrigerated van earlier than expected before heading overseas. It was very likely he would never return. His mobile phone was brimming with unanswered texts and voice mails from the remaining colleagues in the Lake District.

He switched the mobile off - soon he would be on his way for good.

Alice had settled the box of Maddox's belongings on the kitchen table, and taped the keys on top of it. Looking around the sparse rooms, she moved across the kitchen floor, to the freezer, and lifted the lid.

If only it had been possible to settle down with David - the same house and kitchen with Maddox seemed irredeemably sterile and bleak by comparison. Irritably Alice shook the unbidden images from her mind - all she ever wanted was to see those beautiful eyes of David's just one more time.

And then she did.

It would take Maddox a short while to prepare the work for transit - it had to be thorough and precise. It was a pity about the hair but a wig or hairpiece could not be condoned - it would degrade the whole work. If there was a slight chance of a scalp along the way - that would be good, but there were more important things to consider now - a new identity for one. The final joining instructions needed to be downloaded, and confirmation of his passwords was required before setting off.

Maddox clicked open the boot of the car, and hauled out a couple of leather bags - they clinked and sloshed as he carefully laid them on the ground.

Alice reeled back from the freezer, the glass of water shattering on the floor.

The eyes that looked back at her were not popping with laughter, and hadn't been for some time. The frosted lashes were still splayed out like sea anemones, and the cloudy patina of death had failed to entirely mask those beautiful features. But the eyes were David's.

Those wondrous eyes of her beloved were looking out at her - not from across the fabled divide of silken sheets - but from the cushioned setting of some crinkle-cut chips and a bag of sweetcorn.

The information her mind received was vague despite the evidence of her own eyes, as if the whole scene was busy scrabbling around in her brain for a suitable outlet. Fear and shock stole through her, creeping into her bone marrow, dropping lead in her stomach. It seemed only a matter of time for her to wake from this nightmare - this potent mix of half awake, half dream. But they were David's eyes - it was all too vivid and real. Alice could feel everything going black, the walls of the room retracting and expanding. Somewhere, at some level of consciousness, she heard the click of a door.

"Alice?" said Maddox, taking in the scene before him - the opened chest freezer, the buckled knees of Alice, the rucked carpet where she had stumbled backwards in shock, and the bone-white knuckles on the back of a chair.

"Alice - you've dropped your glass," he said.

"David?" she spluttered. "It's David!"

"Well, part of him," Maddox conceded, moving smoothly through to the kitchen area where he set down his luggage. There was a slight tinkle as one of the glass jars leant into a ceramic dish. In the silence, it was like the ringing of a bell.

"After all, it was what he would have wanted," Maddox gestured towards the freezer before turning to the small fridge in the kitchen. "He was an artist as well, you know. He would have approved of his contribution to what could possibly be a new defining era in the world of art."

The light outside was golden and mellow, and streaming through the window it mined the electric blue highlights of Alice's thick, black hair. They were little pinpricks of cobalt, tiny wires of kingfisher blue woven into her raven locks.

"You have beautiful hair," Maddox said. "Thick, shiny and black - absolutely perfect in every way."

He took a syringe and a small glass bottle out of the fridge.

"But why?"

"It's what I do," said Maddox. "I am rather good at it."

Maddox carefully laid the tray down on a small table. He then walked over to the freezer and picked up David's eyes,

233

holding them up to the light to see them better - then gently laid them down on a napkin. They had been so finicky to clean with all that tough, fibrous tissue surrounding them - he was especially pleased with the cutting of the lids to retain the lashes.

They still have the lashes on them, thought Alice.

"Ah, here we are."

Maddox had drawn up a cloudy mixture from the glass vial, and was tapping it gently to disperse the air bubbles.

"We don't want any of these getting into the blood stream," he said.

Alice backed away - David's eyes seemed to follow her around the room.

"Keep away from me," she croaked.

It was pathetic - Alice always seemed incapable of screaming, even as a little girl - a husky croak would never be her salvation.

Maddox moved slowly towards Alice with the syringe held aloft, his manner gentle and reassuring. He was a little conciliatory in his approach - as though he did genuinely regret this course of action, but was unable to avert it.

CHAPTER THIRTY-ONE

How beautiful it was in the end.

Everyone said so.

He submitted the work and called it: Alice.

No one could ever accuse Maddox of being pretentious. Naturally, there had been a few enquiries as to why he had chosen such a title. Some suggestions hinted at an allusion to an elusive wonderland - a looking glass world - a representation of debris from another dimension.

Maddox just smiled and nodded enigmatically - it's what he did - it's what he did best.

The title of his project was probably the least important aspect about the whole enterprise, and over the past year or so, he had given very little thought to branding his work.

But in the end, the title 'Alice' just suited it so very well.

Alice's thick, black hair really was the crowning glory of his achievement. It cushioned the skull perfectly, and wreathed the features in a luscious pitch backdrop, which shone with streaks of cobalt and electric blue. What beautiful hair - glossy, thick and black - it really brought the cheekbones out, and what a fitting tribute to Alice.

If only she could be here to see it.

In the main hall of the exhibition, smaller displays were ranked along the walls, but his own work had been mounted and presented on a central plinth, with subdued lighting. The effect it created was as startling as he ever imagined it would be.

Like a hungry predator circling his prey, Maddox remained close to his creation. There wasn't a single person who didn't pause to gaze upon this wondrous composition of his - this work that had been so long in the making.

He glanced up and could see Corpuscle looking edgy and restless over by his own display - he refused to meet Maddox's eye, and constantly traced his own allotted territory with short, pithy steps.

The judging would begin soon. He would take a walk around the exhibition later perhaps - see what Corpuscle and his main rivals had produced. Corpuscle had the mien of an old lion about to relinquish his pride to a younger, fitter male.

Maddox would take that pride.

Viewers milled around, having been stopped in their tracks at the sight before them. Quick glances at catalogues, many nodding approval, and several deep in thought - a tall, thin man with a white goatee beard stood with his mouth open. An elderly woman, with dry powdered cheeks and a whiskered mole, asked him to name his price.

Maddox would visit the other displays and exhibits soon, but for the time being his own precious work was just too perfect for him to leave.

He wanted to cherish every second of it.

Alice woke up.

She was feeling groggy and her mouth was dry and her lips cracked. She licked her lips but her tongue felt fat and turgid, lying in her mouth like a leather poultice. How long had she been asleep? Slowly, she stood up and shook her head - there were dregs of a dream sloshing around in there - a dream that felt bad and seemed reluctant to leave her. What was she doing in Maddox's apartment?

Something didn't feel quite right.

She had been sleeping on the couch - a blanket had been pulled snuggly around her, a quilt covered her legs. Her head felt cold. Head throbbing and feeling nauseous, she staggered to the bathroom, hands ready to pounce on any furniture lest she suddenly feel dizzy. Clutching the sink, Alice spun the tap to get a glass of water, letting it run for a few seconds but it never really got cold. Bowed over, feeling so ill, she was then violently sick.

She didn't need to hold the hair out of her eyes.

She stopped retching, and raised her head to look in the mirror. On a small stool by the sink, and still plugged in, were some hair clippers. Tiny tufts of glossy, thick black hair were curled around the clippers - glossy and black with glinting blue highlights.

At first, all that would come out of her would be a low, dull croak.

Then she would begin to scream.

ABOUT THE AUTHOR

John Crawford is a freelance writer, illustrator and
cartoonist from the West Midlands.
When he isn't doodling or scribbling, he is usually
subjecting his very dodgy knees to long walks and playing
football. Either that or just heading off to the pub.
Fuelled by chocolate, he has published numerous articles,
cartoons and illustrations over the years.

36475253R00146

Made in the USA
Charleston, SC
05 December 2014